The Windless Sky

Michael Owens

Pepperback Press, Inc.

Contents

1

The edge of everything

It was time to dismantle her life on Earth. Sitting in a little coffee shop near the i-port, Maisy started going through her tabs. One of the benefits of being an introvert was that no one noticed when you abruptly disappeared from the face of the planet.

She hit the unsub link at the top of her sophomore class board. Maisy scrolled through the farm girl posts, chickens in sweaters and seasonal growing plans and heated arguments over non-toxic grub deterrents. *Unsub.* The board where locals posted live events in a town five hundred miles away that she'd never see again. *Unsub.* Recycled art. *Unsub.* Lost and found pets of Franklin County. *Unsub. Unsub. Unsub.*

Earth. *Unsub.*

It was midmorning when Maisy looked up from her tablet. The cafe was bustling and it was time to buy something or leave the table for a paying customer. She did both, grabbing a bagel from the autochef and heading back out onto the street. Maisy had one more item on her mom's bucket list. Heading further west along the platform, she slipped onto a ramp moving up.

The best museums were clustered two levels up, along the edge of the new harbor. Rebuilt about ten years after the last big terrorist attacks, the new heart of the city had been funded by big corporate sponsors and their logos were worked into the sides of the buildings and ramps, even the platforms themselves.

Transitioning from the Suki-Nyberg quad into the neighboring Dynatech enclave there was a definite change in aesthetic. SN was all pale blue and glass and the buildings themselves tended to be flat and featureless. DT was a much more dynamic, modern vibe. The buildings here had multifaceted exteriors that featured weird angles and vibrant colors. Maisy passed under a pool suspended between two towers, scantily clad bodies visible from below. It was definitely an interesting look and made the enclave a nice place to visit, but she wouldn't want to live here.

The lunch time pedestrian traffic had picked up by the time Maisy reached her destination. The New Museum of Western Art was a typical DT building, primarily red and yellow; it stretched up into the level above it and was set back from the platform foot traffic lanes with a large glass atrium trimmed in blue.

The interior of the building was visible from the walkway and Maisy was relieved to note that it didn't seem overly crowded. Walking through the main doors, a large holo-sign displayed an image of her target, rotating to a 3D map of the building displaying an illuminated path. *Well, that was easy.*

Maisy's goal was holding court in the center of the museum's largest gallery. A school group was clustered before the enigmatic Italian woman, the children jumping and chatting irreverently as she hovered slightly above them.

As the group finally moved on, Maisy claimed the bench directly across from Da Vinci's masterpiece and sat with her roller bag between her feet and her hands folded in her lap.

Seeing this painting in person was the last item on her mom's list. The last thing Maisy had to do, on her last day on the planet. When her mom asked her to go to the rim, she'd already prepared a list of things she wanted Maisy to do first. Some of the items on the bucket list were things that her mom had done as a teenager in the city that she wanted Maisy to get to do. Some of them, like this one, were things her mom had never had the chance to do.

And would never get the chance to do.

Her mom had only had twenty-four days between her diagnosis and her last breath. Not enough time for fun day trips. Barely enough time to find homes for the animals and make arrangements for all of their things to be sold, including the farm. Liquidation, as the lawyer referred to it.

And just enough time to bounce a message to the rim and get confirmation back that Maisy had a place waiting for her there. A place with a man she only remembered from photographs, who was technically her father but felt like a stranger.

The face of the unfazed woman in the painting hanging before her was more familiar to Maisy than her own father's. Jackson Renner had made appearances in the old fashioned photo album stuffed in her backpack, but neither his face nor his name had been part of their lives.

She stared into the painting's gaze. Not quite a smile. The woman seemed resigned to her fate.

Sighing, Maisy stood from the bench and moved back toward the front of the museum to hail a taxi. Her mother's bucket list was done. The last thing she'd promised her, or rather the second to last.

The last thing would be getting on the transport.

The autocar pulled up in front of the tower facade of the i-port at ten minutes before noon and the door slid open. Maisy grabbed her backpack and rolling bag from the seat beside her and stepped out of the driverless vehicle. The terminal's glass doors whooshed open as she approached..

Maisy had checked in online from the hotel that morning, so she ignored the check-in desks and followed the signs to security. There was no line and she walked into one of the open black boxes. The doors slid shut behind her and the lights dimmed. Her reflection in the glass wall sharpened and several points glowed red. Green text appeared beside her reflection.

_ *Maisy Dylan Renner*

_ *CLEARED*

The red highlight around her reflection's wrist pulsed once and turned green.

_ *Wrist Unit*

_ *CLEARED*

The red shape marking her backpack pulsed green.

_ *Tablet*

_ *CLEARED*

The final red shape pulsed but stayed red.

_ *Weapon*

Maisy held very still as her reflection disappeared, leaving just the image of the bag, which increased in size. The exterior of the bag became transparent and a 3D rendering of the contents was visible on the glass wall. Everything disappeared except a small old fashioned pocket knife. Finally, the outline pulsed to green.

_ *Blade less than 6cm*

_ *CLEARED*

The wall on the opposite side of the box slid open and Maisy took a deep breath before walking out into the bright terminal lights. She moved slowly, giving her eyes a moment to adjust. The large panel up ahead displayed her name and her cabin number, and a blue arrow pointing to the right. A matching arrow appeared on the floor at her feet and Maisy followed it down a large, wide hallway. The arrows continued to appear before her as she walked deeper and deeper into the i-port.

As Maisy crossed the rubber seal connecting the ship to the terminal, the air cooled and the flatweave carpet abruptly ended. The ship's decking was some kind of textured alloy with a nonslip coating. It reminded Maisy of the composite boards that she and her mom had looked at when they needed to repair their kitchen floor last year. In the end they'd decided against them. Instead, they'd cannibalized the old potting shed. Like land, real wood was hard to come by these days.

Maisy turned into a long hallway full of doors. Ahead of her, other passengers were entering their rooms. Couples and families hustled into their spots, doors closing behind them. Further down the hall the doors were set closer together into the wall, the units smaller.

A door flashed blue ahead and slid open. The small room had just enough space for a person to stand beside the single cot. Another cot was set in the wall above the first that could be flipped down into position if needed. Half of the space was taken up by a bath unit. All the comforts of home. Maisy glanced over her shoulder and watched the door close silently behind her.

After using the small bathroom, Maisy pulled her brush from her bag and smoothed her curls up onto a topknot. She knew when she took it down, her hair would fall right back into place. Her mother joked that their hair only did one thing, but it did it well.

People who saw them together always mentioned how much they looked alike, and Maisy loved to hear that. But she knew it was mostly the hair. Her mother's brown eyes were warm like whiskey. Maisy's were so dark there was little sign of where the pupils began. Her mother's face was golden, no matter the season. Maisy was pale, and the sharp shadows cast by her cheekbones made her skin seem even paler.

She'd seen the pictures of Jackson Renner. It was his face that stared back at her when she looked in the mirror.

A low musical tone rang through the small cabin and a female voice announced ten minutes to launch. The cabin door flashed red and the panel beside it indicated that it was locked for take off. Maisy took a long, calming breath.

Warning. All passengers please enter assigned berths. The transport will launch in five minutes.

She stowed both of her bags under the bed and lowered herself onto the cot. The moment her body settled into the mattress the foamcore warmed and molded to her shape. The ceiling above the bed flashed green and displayed the launch countdown. As she watched the numbers change, Maisy's body grew heavy and the lights in the cabin dimmed. Somewhere far beneath her, the ship's engines rumbled and faint vibrations tingled through her fingertips.

Or maybe that was the cryofield kicking in...

Maisy lost her train of thought as her eyes drifted closed. She imagined the ship pulling away from the gravity of the planet and a single tear left a track across her temple and disappeared into her hair as she drifted into sleep.

They said you weren't supposed to dream in cryosleep.

The sun was warm on her skin and the sky was a vivid blue above her, but none of it was real. Her mother sat beside her in one of the old plastic lawn chairs they kept on their front porch, smiling her lopsided smile, one eyebrow raised.

The hand resting on the white plastic began to melt.

Skin dripped down like paint from her fingers, then her arms and shoulders. Her dark, curly hair, just like Maisy's, flowed like ink. As Maisy sat there and watched, even her mother's smile slipped down onto the weathered gray boards of the porch and disappeared until only the chair remained.

Maisy opened her eyes without moving any other part of her body and took stock of her surroundings. Her mother always accused her of waking up like a cat. Waking up from three months of cryosleep was apparently no different.

Welcome to the Citadel was flashing on the ceiling above her with a countdown to docking. Maisy sat up, stiff and woozy. A canister of water slid out from the panel at the head of the cot and she drank it down obediently. By the time she'd stretched her tight muscles and used the small bathroom, the door had flashed green and there were sounds of movement from the hallway.

Slipping into her backpack, she pulled her roller bag behind her as she exited the tiny cabin. She merged into the flow of passengers following the green arrows leading them from the ship to the station.

As she approached the gate her name flashed beside a blue arrow, which she followed through the arrivals terminal to a small crowd of men and women in the black and gray fatigues of s-marines.

They all wore the same monochromatic camo pants. Some wore matching jackets over black t-shirts or tanks, all variations on a theme. Her eyes were drawn to the tall dark-haired man in the center of the group. The woman next to him was punching him on the arm and he was laughing. A dark arm snaked around his shoulders from the other side and the tall uniformed man next to him rocked him off his feet for a second. The group of five or six people were laughing and chatting loudly as the other passengers walking past gave them a wide berth.

Jackson Renner hadn't changed much in the ten years since he'd left Earth. His hair was still dark and thick. He had a lean runner's build, with no sign of a middle-age paunch. As she got closer Maisy noted that his pale skin was clear and his eyes still dark and sharp. Her mother had always looked younger than her age as well, until the very end. Maisy stamped down a flash of anger and took a deep breath. There was no point in wishing for impossible things.

She walked up to the group and stopped in front of Jackson, who was chatting with the dark-skinned man to his right.

"Hi, I'm Maisy." *Smooth.*

Conversation skittered to a halt as the group all whipped their heads in her direction. She ignored everyone else, staring at her father. His throat moved as he swallowed and suddenly she was engulfed in warm, solid arms, her face pressed against a black-clothed chest.

Maisy's eyes burned as her father pressed his face into her hair and his breath was warm against her ear as he said, "I'm so sorry about your mom."

She imagined pushing him away and screaming at him for pretending to care about her or her mom when he was nothing more than a stranger. She had a vision of herself crying and clinging to him like a toddler, tears and snot running down her face. She wanted to cut him dead, thank him calmly and coolly walk away, leaving him to trail behind in confusion and hurt. But she couldn't manage any of those.

In the end, she was just tired.

Maisy struggled not to sag as a wave of exhaustion rolled over her. She patted Jackson awkwardly on the back and gently disengaged herself from his embrace.

"Thanks." She swallowed and cleared her throat. "Thank you for meeting me."

Jackson stepped back and held her firmly by the shoulders, taking in her gaunt face and shadowed eyes. Wheels were moving behind his eyes and he sighed, turning to his friends with his arm around her shoulder.

"Let me introduce you to this motley crew, so you know who to avoid around here." The three men and one woman were very different, despite their similar dress.

Gesturing toward the tall Black man, Jackson introduced, "Gray is my right hand man. His middle name is trouble, though." Jackson punched his friend on the arm and Maisy thought, *oh god he's a toucher*. Her dad's friend held out his hand and Maisy shook it briefly.

"Nice to meet you," she said, dredging up a smile.

Gray smiled, the corners of his eyes crinkling. His hand was huge and warm and dry. "It's a pleasure to meet you, Maisy. We're all very happy to have you here." Gray seemed about the same age as her dad and nearly the same height, but his shoulders were much broader and his head was perfectly, gleamingly bald.

The shorter blond man next to him extended his hand eagerly. As Maisy took it he covered her hand with his other and leaned forward conspiratorially. "I'm Joe. And Gray's middle name is trouble because he's so good at getting us all out of it." Joe winked and released Maisy, who was already well on her way to becoming shellshocked. Joe had gray in his blond hair upon closer inspection but he seemed younger than the other two. Maisy wondered absently if it was just his lack of height that made her think he was younger.

The third man was taller than Joe, but definitely the youngest by far and closer to Maisy's age than that of her father and his friends.

"This is Tal, our resident magician," Jackson introduced. Tal was maybe a centimeter shorter than Jackson with a shock of light brown hair that sprang from his head like fur, thick and unruly. He clasped Maisy's hand briefly and gave her a crooked smile. "Engineer," he said.

Jackson shook his head and clapped a hand on the younger man's shoulder. "Nope. Certified magician," he smiled. "And this is Ann, our pilot." Ann had a bright red pixie cut and her cheeks matched as Jackson pulled her into a one armed hug, Maisy still anchored to his other side.

Ann extended her hand to Maisy across Jackson's chest and offered an apologetic smile. "And den mother. They have an average mental age of about twelve."

A chorus of denials sprung up around them but Maisy and Ann shared a look acknowledging the truth of her statement.

"It's really great to meet you all," Maisy said as honestly as she could.

Ann nudged Jackson in the ribs. "Let's get back to G deck and get Maisy some dinner, Jackson."

Maisy's dad unhooked his arm from Ann and reached down to grab Maisy's roller bag and pass it to Tal, then he slid her backpack from her shoulder and swung it onto his own. Draping his left arm over her shoulder again, Jackson steered Maisy back into the stream of passengers flooding into the station.

"It's a little early for dinner by station time, but I know you haven't really eaten for three months, so we're going to introduce you to the Big Tow."

Maisy was still trying to resign herself to the touching and it took her a moment to process what Jackson was saying.

"The Big Toe?" she asked, trying to sound more interested than she felt.

"Yup! Tow as in T-O-W, as in an old tug that used to move the big freighters around the terminal. They turned it into a restaurant on G deck. You'll love it."

Maisy doubted that—a lot—but she allowed herself to be ushered out of the terminal and into an open atrium.

They appeared to be on the mid deck of the station and balconies stretched up and down. There was a light source up there somewhere. Below the decks were bustling with activity and what looked like storefronts, restaurants, and hallways branched off deeper into the station.

Their small group approached the glide running along the inside of the balcony and stepped onto the spiral heading down. Maisy allowed the conversation to flow past her and took in each deck as they passed by.

The Citadel was run by Citatech and Maisy noted their black and yellow branding everywhere. Even the people who populated the decks and rode the glides were outfitted in black, with flashes of yellow here and there. Maisy looked down at her black cargo pants, dark gray tee, and black long-sleeve shirt. She fit right in.

The other passengers disembarking from the transport were a fairly diverse crowd. The younger passengers tended to dress casually, like Maisy, while older passengers dressed conservatively in sweater sets and button down shirts. The business passengers sported black suits with black, gray, or white shirts. Workers seemed to wear black or gray overalls. The few s-marines in the crowd were dressed like her dad and his friends.

As they moved further down to the lower decks the crowds were changing. They exited the glide on G deck and the families and business suits had pretty much disappeared. This level seemed mostly overalls and fatigues.

The banter between Jackson and his friends passed over Maisy's head as she took in her surroundings. The station seemed to be laid out in a circular pattern. Wide hallways shot off like spokes from the atrium, with storefronts on either side and kiosks or carts scattered between. The ceilings were high enough that there were balconies above some of the storefronts. They passed an alcove off the main hallway that looked like a tiny park with seating areas scattered around what were obviously fake trees. A short distance down the hall on the opposite side was another alcove.

As they turned into it, Maisy stumbled a bit in shock to see a small ship sitting on the deck.

The port tug was about twice the length of a city bus and just as wide. It filled the two story alcove from floor to ceiling. The hatch in the center of the side of the ship was open and plasta-crete stairs had been placed up to the entrance. As a tug, the rectangular ship had been outfitted with ports across the entire front deck so that the crew could easily maneuver around the terminal and assist the big transports and freighters into their docks. Now all of those screens had been removed and Maisy looked into the belly of the small ship. The interior appeared to have been completely gutted and was set up with rows of tables and a long bar.

"Wow." Maisy shook her head. "Honestly, I just assumed you were insane when you said it was a ship." At her shoulder

Jackson burst out laughing. He pulled her to him and landed a quick kiss on her temple before leading her up the stairs and into the makeshift restaurant. Maisy swallowed and allowed herself to be manhandled into a chair at a round table, her father and his friends crowding around. They leaned elbows on the table. *No personal space issues here*, she thought. Above the tables, large metal-bladed fans spun lazily from the ceiling.

An older man with a ring of gray hair around his head set an old-fashioned pitcher filled with water and a collection of cloudy tumblers in the center of the table.

"Thanks, Sal," Jackson said. "This is my daughter, Maisy." Jackson beamed at the man who smiled back.

"Welcome to the Citadel, Maisy. You look just like your dad."

Jackson barked out a laugh. "No need to be rude, Sal."

Sal shook his head, chuckling as he bustled off.

Gray, seated on Maisy's left, took command of the pitcher and filled the glasses, handing the first one to Maisy.

"No canisters?" Maisy asked, taking the glass.

"They probably have some up top," Gray told her, "but down here it's a closed system and everything comes through the cyclers."

"Up top?" Maisy asked, then answered her own question. "The upper decks of the station, you mean?"

Joe took a glass from Gray and leaned forward. "Yeah, it's a different world up there."

Maisy sipped her water, relieved to find it cool. The overhead fans stirred the air, moving it over her skin.

"Is it always this warm in here?" Maisy asked.

Joe nodded, sipping his water. "Yeah, down here it is. This isn't too bad. It gets worse as you get closer to the core."

Tal took a glass from Gray and leaned forward across the table. "The station's core is a modified power plant that processes the raw ore brought in by the system miners. The excess heat from the refinement process is used to power the station and the refined ore is sent back to Earth. The ambient temperature is optimized for the outermost decks of the station, where the Citatech management has their offices and living spaces. The rest of the station's inhabitants are assigned decks based on their place in the corporate hierarchy—"

Tal seemed ready to launch into a dissertation on the socio-cultural constructs of interstellar commercial habitations but Ann slapped him on the back of the head. The tips of his ears turned red as he sank back in his chair.

"Sometimes the kid needs a hard reset," Ann smiled, sipping her water.

"How do the space marines fit into the corporate structure?" Maisy asked, genuinely curious.

Ann grimaced and set her glass on the table. "Well, as of last week we're technically no longer s-marines." The men's faces all echoed her expression.

"Citatech bought out our contracts from the coalition government," Jackson explained. "But don't you believe that. They may change the patches on our uniforms, but we are still marines, to the bone." There were nods around the table but the faces were definitely unhappy.

"I'm too tired to process what that means," Maisy told him. Jackson smiled and ruffled her hair as if she were a toddler.

"Don't worry about it, kiddo. Let's get some food into you and then right to bed, ok?"

"That sounds good."

Sal appeared at Jackson's elbow with a platter of breaded and fried protein strips, fries, and a stack of white plates. He sat both on the table and turned away. Maisy hadn't seen anyone place an order, but Ann took a plate for herself and placed one in front of Jackson and passed the stack to Tal. The others each took one and Gray handed the last to Maisy. She took the plate and set it down on the table in front of her and contemplated the crispy, greasy food. She was hungry, but was she that hungry?

The others had no such reservations and began dragging fried strips of food from the platter to their plates and diving in. Maisy girded her loins and plucked a strip from the platter and bit off the end. It seemed to be at least a third breading, but it was definitely edible.

The conversation drifted around Maisy as she tucked into what was probably the least healthy meal she'd ever had in her life. The reconstituted texture of the synthetic protein substitute left a weird coating on the roof of her mouth.

Washing it down with water, Maisy decided she'd had enough. Either she hadn't really been that hungry or the lack of actual living matter in the meal had killed her appetite. Either way she was ready to find a bed and crash for another three months. She tuned back into the discussion at the table to estimate how long that might take.

"You guys are fooling yourselves," Joe was shaking his head as he leaned back from the table. Jackson's expression was tight. "Have you even tried to read the e-file? It's a joke. We're no better off than the sanitation bots on this rock. Worse, maybe."

Ann was visibly upset while Gray and Jackson seemed tense and unhappy. Maisy turned to Jackson, "So the s-marines now work for the corporation?"

Jackson sighed and ran his hand down his face. "Yeah, basically. The coalition government has sold the rim—or at least quadrant alpha-seven—to Citatech and it's their problem now. I suspect it was just too hard for the bureaucrats to manage from so far away. With the raiders out here, it just wasn't feasible. So—"

"Wait, what?" Maisy cut him off. "Raiders? Like space pirates?" At this point it would make more sense if she were actually hearing things.

"Yeah, basically. Each of the quadrants out here was licensed to a corp. There were always hostile takeovers—which is why we were stationed out here to begin with—but over the last couple of years it's gotten pretty bad. Corporations sponsored raiding parties who made life difficult for the politicians back home...so they finally threw up their hands and sold the quadrants outright to the corps." Jackson grimaced.

"So what does that mean for you guys?" Maisy asked.

"It means that our enlistments were converted to employment contracts," Jackson started. "We now all officially work for Citatech Security Services."

"Try indentured servitude," Joe interjected. "We were screwed, and they didn't even buy us dinner first."

"It's all just corp-babble. Nothing will change for us," Gray tried to console him, but Joe was becoming agitated.

"You guys aren't paying attention. I keep trying to tell you, you got to read the fine print. They've got us over a barrel, man." Joe leaned back from the table again, running his hands through his thinning hair. Gray patted him on the arm, trying to calm him down.

"Hey, guys. Maisy is beat and this is all too much for her to take in on her first day." Ann looked worried but shot Maisy a smile.

Jackson patted Ann's hand and pushed his chair back to stand. "You're right! Hey, kid, let's get you settled in and let you get some sleep. Tomorrow is another day." Jackson slung Maisy's backpack over his shoulder before grabbing her roller bag. "Thanks, guys. I'll see you all at 0900 at the bay. Try not to get into too much trouble between now and then, okay?"

The tension forgotten, Jackson and his friends shared a round of goodbyes that included way too many punched shoulders and slapped arms. But within minutes Maisy was walking down another wide hallway as her dad led the way.

They turned down one white hallway then another, the passages getting narrower and narrower, until there was barely enough room for the two of them to walk side by side. The doors here were set about two meters apart, recessed into the walls. Finally Jackson stopped at a door and tapped his wrist unit to retract the panel. It slid to the side and he gestured for Maisy to precede him into the tiny space.

Jackson's quarters were narrow, but tall and deep. A thin set of stairs projected from the right hand wall and Maisy realized the handles on the side meant each step was actually a drawer. At the top of the steps was a loft area with a low partition wall blocking her view. A couch ran along the left wall opposite the stairs. Below the loft was a galley kitchen and a small bath unit. Jackson crowded into the tiny living space behind her and Maisy moved into the kitchen and turned around.

"I know it's a lot smaller than what you're used to, Maze." She glanced at him quickly and then looked away, pushing down the memories associated with her mom's nickname for her. "I moved my stuff down here," Jackson continued, "and the loft is all yours." He moved to the side so she could climb the steep, narrow staircase. Perched atop the tiny platform was a miniature bedroom with a bunk, bookcases, and a small closet. It was more than Maisy had expected, given the tight space.

"This is awesome. Thank you," she told her father sincerely.

"I know this has been hard. All of it." Jackson met Maisy's eyes where she stood near the top of the steps. "We'll get through it together, kid. You're not alone." Maisy took her backpack from her dad and tossed it onto the bed at the top of the stairs and reached back down to accept the roller bag. She hefted it onto the platform and it took up about half of the floorspace, but she wasn't going to complain. A grown man had committed to sleeping on his couch indefinitely, so she was going to keep her mouth shut. For tonight at least.

Maneuvering around her bag to sit on the bed, Maisy realized she had total privacy. She quickly pulled a pair of sleep shorts from her bag and changed. Stepping carefully back down the narrow staircase, Maisy found her dad had set up the couch as a bed and changed as well. Poking around the kitchen she found an old fashioned pitcher of water in the cooler and glasses in the cabinet above the sink. She poured herself a glass of water and shimmied back up to her cubby hole.

"Goodnight, Maze," her dad called out. A moment later the main lights in the unit gently darkened until only a narrow band of faint illumination remained at the top and bottom of each wall so that she wouldn't kill herself on the stairs if she had to pee in the middle of the night.

Maisy hesitated a moment, considering her options.

"Goodnight, Dad." Maisy pulled her legs under the thin blanket on her bunk and tucked her hand under her pillow. A moment later, she was asleep.

2

Welcome to the rim

Maisy closed the panel for bio class and set the tablet on the bed beside her. After two weeks of using the station's EDU modules, Maisy realized she was starting to miss having a live instructor—but she did enjoy being able to move through the coursework at her own pace. The sounds of movement came from the kitchen below and the warm, spicy scent of breakfast was working its way to her loft. It almost smelled like meat, but that was the one thing she was positive it wasn't.

In all fairness, she'd been rather impressed with the meals Jackson had produced over the past two weeks. Her father was surprisingly domesticated and he was making a real effort to ease her transition to station life.

"What mystery mess have you prepared for us today?" She descended her tiny staircase as Jackson looked up from the plate he was pulling from the small cooker installed in the upper cabinets.

"Set up the table for us and you'll find out." Jackson shoveled half of the food onto another plate and reached down to the cooler set under the counter to pull out the pitcher of cold water.

Maisy flipped the tabletop down from its dock in the wall of the tiny living room and took a seat on the couch. Jackson set the pitcher and two glasses on the surface, took two steps back to the postage stamp kitchen to grab the plates, set those on the table, and pulled the bench from below the staircase over to the other side. Taking his seat he slid one of the plates over to Maisy while she poured water into each glass.

Passing her dad his glass, Maisy smiled. "Well, it doesn't smell burned..."

"Damned by faint praise," Jackson sighed.

"...this time." Maisy finished.

Jackson

After breakfast, Jackson grabbed his bag from a hook by the door. "I'm meeting the team for a training exercise, but we'll be back by 1700 and head over to the Big Tow for dinner. Meet us there?"

He swung his bag onto his shoulder and turned to look at his daughter. She was still pale but the past weeks had lightened the shadows under her eyes. She was making an effort to fit into station life. He knew it and he appreciated it.

Jackson walked to the door and glanced back at Maisy, surprised to find her on his heels. "Don't you have school today?"

"I've finished all of my assignments for the week. It's not exactly rocket science."

"Is it too easy? Did they place you wrong?"

"It's just easy enough that I don't have to think about it. And that's what I need right now," Maisy said firmly. She hiked her bag over her shoulder and moved past him and into the hallway.

She turned back with a small smile. "I'm heading to the park on B deck. I'll see you later at the Tow." Maisy turned away and walked with purpose toward the center of the station.

Jackson shook his head and walked slowly in the other direction, thinking. *Discretion being the better part of valor...* He was content to let the matter lie for the moment. Maisy and her mom had been two peas in a pod, but he'd realized over the past months that Maisy was indeed as much his daughter as she was Mary's. They'd fallen into a surprisingly easy rhythm. Jackson had struggled with serious concerns about sharing his small living space with a moody teenage girl. Instead he'd gotten a tidy, polite roommate who shared his sense of humor.

Swinging into the beta dock on the dark side of the station, Jackson spotted his team prepping their corvette, the *Windless Sky*. It wasn't much bigger than the old tug they had dinner in, but the *Sky* packed a hell of a punch. She was agile and armed to the teeth. Joe and Tal were threading missiles in through the port hatch as Jackson approached. Tal smiled. "Last one, Captain! These new rounds are all upgraded with the 7.2 firmware release. Increased velocity by three point five percent according to the release notes!"

Jackson shook his head at the engineer's enthusiasm. "Thanks, Kid. Is Ann on board?"

Tal nodded as he maneuvered the munitions hatch closed and secured it. Joe wiped the white silicone grease from his hands onto a rag and flung it over his shoulder. "That's it. Let's go burn some fuel."

"Damn straight," Jackson replied. The three of them lurched up the ramp and into the ship's hull. Jackson and Joe headed to the bridge and Tal stopped at the door to retract the ramp and secure the main hatch.

Tal

Tal joined the rest of the crew on the bridge a moment later, sliding into his station across from Gray.

Green lights shone straight across the board and Tal initiated his training simulation protocol. He also ran two test scripts in the background that he'd been working on. There was always a percentage point here and there to squeeze out of the systems. And you never knew when that could make the difference in a firefight. Since joining Jackson and the crew of the *Sky* six months ago, Tal had seen more real action than he ever could have imagined back on Earth, graduating with a degree in interstellar engineering. Joining the s-marines had given him the opportunity to get real world experience and do work that made a difference.

At the center of the bridge, Jackson had assumed the command chair and was going through the launch sequence with Ann. Tal confirmed all systems green for engineering and Gray gave the weapons status. Joe bantered with the traffic officer and minutes later they were cleared to exit the bay.

Ann took them up gently, hovering above the deck and moving to the main tower shaft. Then they were rising up the shaft to the surface of the asteroid that formed the foundation of the Citadel.

This section of the rock was barren, but as they exited the shaft and swung up and around, the crew had a view of the dome that made up the roof of the uppermost decks of the station, gleaming like a silver eye in the rock's craggy face.

Tal admired the amazing feat of engineering that the Citadel represented. Carved from an asteroid with a titanium core, Citatech had built their flagship station to serve as a jumping off point for all of their operations in the quadrant. From the Citadel, the corporation launched mining operations and colonial expeditions, and directed commercial traffic be-

tween the adjacent quadrants, the outposts beyond the fron-
tier, and Earth.

And until recently, the Citadel had also hosted the s-marine
outpost for the quadrant. Now there were no more space
marines. Tal had enlisted for a five year term and still had
nearly four years in his contract—which now belonged to
Citatech. They still weren't sure exactly what that meant.

Rumors abounded. Joe was trying to convince everyone
that the corporations were going to start harvesting their or-
gans at any moment, but the escalation of raider activity in
the mining belt had kept most of them too busy to obsess
over the bureaucracy and politics. No matter who signed their
checks or what they called them, the crew of the *Sky* were still
s-marines and they had a job to do.

Two commercial freighters had been lost in the last month.
They'd found debris from one and the official conclusion was
that it had gone down with all hands on board. The other
was still missing. A J-class heavy freighter, twenty-seven crew
members, and eight point three billion dollars of ore were all
just gone, lost somewhere between an orbital mining platform
in sector 7 and the Citadel. It was a lot of space to cover and
there were only three corvettes assigned to the station.

Tal knew that Jackson had requested another team from the
station's executive director, and management claimed more
resources were on the way, but everyone was on edge at the
moment.

"Looking good, guys." Jackson interrupted Tal's train of
thought as the *Sky* entered her standard elliptical trajectory
away from the launch shaft. "Let's put these new rounds to the
test and work out any kinks. Ann, have you got the run plotted
for us?"

The redheaded pilot nodded and tapped her console to
engage the heads up display. A neon track was overlaid on the
star chart. "We're going to use the S3 asteroid cluster for target
practice today. The ore in that belt is completely played out

and the installation was stripped down and abandoned last year." Ann hit a few keys on her console and the screen to the right of the main view lit up with a zoomed in view of the asteroid belt. Three larger rocks were tagged, one obviously housing the abandoned facility.

Tal pulled up the data on the asteroid cluster and the facility on his own screen and checked the density and composition. "This is great, Ann! We can test the new rounds on the two main types of rock in this belt and also on the alloy composite walls of the facility." Joe rolled his eyes from his seat at comms, but the captain was smiling.

"It's all yours, Ann!" Jackson told the pilot and turned his smile to Tal. "Let's go blow some stuff up, Kid."

"Hell, yeah!" Tal shouted before he could stop himself. But the captain was laughing and even Joe seemed to be in a better mood. Gray watched them all indulgently, shaking his head.

Ann initiated the jump and the main screen flickered. One second the display was showing the curtain of stars around the station and the next the view had changed to just outside the asteroid belt.

Tal's stomach caught up with them a split second later. He swallowed hard and the sensation passed. Some people reacted much more strongly to interstellar hops—and they usually figured out quickly that a life among the stars was not for them.

Tal accessed his console to compare the readings on the mothballed facility with the information in his database. The short range scanners confirmed the composite materials but a large metallic object popped up at the edge of the array. Narrowing the focus, he furrowed his brow.

"Captain, there's a ship out there." Tal swiped the data from his console to one of the secondary panels and tagged the position. "Right there. It reads big, at least a freighter."

Jackson rose and walked up to the screen, tapping the surface to zoom in as far as he could. They were still too far out to make out anything more than the gleam of a metallic surface.

Gray voiced everyone's thoughts. "Our missing freighter?"

"Let's find out." Jackson answered, returning to his seat.

Ann engaged the main thrusters and the *Sky* started moving toward the belt. "ETA seven minutes but we should be able to ID it in half that."

"I'm working on it," Tal responded. He pulled up the specifications for the missing ship and slid them onto the other secondary panel.

The screen on the left showed the zoomed in view on the object in front of them and the screen on the right now displayed the image of the *Cerulean Sailing Star*, a Suki-Nyberg leased freighter missing from a mining run three sectors away. The ship was a huge, rectangular warehouse with engines slapped onto one of its short ends. It was utilitarian and just plain ugly to Tal's eye. But these big freighters got the job done, moving huge loads from point A to point B. Usually.

Within minutes Tal was almost positive they were looking at the same ship, but there were no power signatures. At the comms station, Joe was trying to hail the crew and checking the bands for distress signals or transponder IDs.

"There's no signal of any kind, including ID, coming off that ship," Joe said, his voice tight.

Jackson rose from his chair again to approach the zoomed in view of the ship. "Ann, can you swing us around to see if we can get a visual hull ID?" Everyone was silent as the *Sky* angled in toward the much larger ship.

"There it is," Tal snapped a frame of the current view and froze it on the left secondary screen. *Cerulean Sailing Star* was emblazoned on the side of the freighter near the bow, with a sixteen digit ID number below. Tal double checked the ID number but there was no doubt this was the missing ship.

Maisy shut down her tablet and slipped it back into her bag. She rested her arms across the tops of her pulled up knees and glanced at the families strolling along the paved pathways. No one else was sitting on the artificial grass and Maisy had received several odd looks as the Cits passed her.

There had been too many other things going on for Maisy to do more than a cursory search on the Citadel before leaving Earth, but she'd spent the last couple months making up for that. Her first discovery, that Citatech was censoring the data available to residents of the station, had been alarming.

They were three months away from the nearest live net connection and that meant they were dependent on downloads carried on transports from Earth. The moment a ship left the system, the data was old. Worse, the download only encompassed the named—aka *legal*—sections of the internet. Ninety-nine percent of the net was outside the government regulated naming system and accessed via ever-changing IP addresses. Residents of the Citadel had zero access to unsanctioned data.

Given the limits on the data accessible, it was telling that the management of Citatech had apparently decided it was necessary to censor even that already filtered data. What could they possibly be afraid the Cits would access? Lucky for Maisy, the effort to censor the data was being done in the laziest ways possible. There were so many dead ends that they created a crystal clear picture of what was missing, if anyone cared to look.

Unfortunately for Citatech, Maisy was bored. Mapping the missing data and analyzing the pattern of censorship had become her new hobby. Some of the blackouts were obvious—for example there was no mention of the missing ships that her dad and his team were worried about. Others seemed almost random. It would be interesting to figure out if there were some suitably dramatic deep dark conspiracy or if it were simple incompetence and paranoia at play.

Maisy guessed the latter.

A beep from her wrist unit reminded Maisy of her promise to meet Jackson at the diner, so she pushed herself to her feet. It was habit to brush at her black cargo pants, despite the fact that she knew there was no actual dirt in the park. Real dirt was a precious commodity in space and reserved for the hydroponics sector on the top deck of the station.

Another well-dressed Cit family gave Maisy a funny look as she crossed to the paved walkway and made her way out of the artificial park and back to the main atrium. No one here stepped off the path.

Their loss, Maisy thought.

As Maisy entered the glide down to the lower decks the lights dimmed. She looked up at the ceiling, frowning. It wasn't her imagination. The illumination was steadily decreasing as she descended through the decks.

Well, that's new.

The change was subtle and only noticeable as you went down the glide from deck to deck. Once she exited the glide and left the atrium behind, her eyes adjusted. She never would have known the lower deck was dimmer if she hadn't seen the difference from the glide.

As Maisy approached the retrofitted tug that housed the Big Tow, she scanned the growing traffic for Jackson and the other members of the *Sky*'s crew. It was shift change for most of the inhabitants of the station and the deck was crowded with jumpsuits. The Tow was starting to fill up, so Maisy grabbed a table and pulled out her tablet to wait. Sal, the owner, maître d', head waiter, and bus boy, smiled her way but left her alone.

Maisy was using a stylus to manipulate her dimensional database when she spotted her dad and his crew at the door. Waving them over, Maisy caught Sal's eye and he hustled over with a pitcher and glasses. The five marines pulled up their chairs to the table and sat staring down at the surface.

By end of shift—especially an end of shift on time—the *Sky*'s crew was usually boisterous to the point of being annoying. The longer they sat there quietly, no one making eye contact, the more concerned Maisy became. If they weren't all present she'd think there had been a horrible accident on the run today.

Sal came back to the table with food, glancing at the quiet faces and the untouched pitcher and glasses. He and Maisy shared a look and she shrugged. Sal had been on the station long enough to know better than to ask. As he walked away, Maisy caught Jackson's eye and arched a brow.

Jackson shook his head and cleared his throat. "How was the park, Maze?"

"It was fine," she replied. "How was your training run?" She scanned the faces of the team, looking for the weak link. "Hey Tal, how did your new rounds perform?"

Tal started at being called out. "Um...we didn't actually get to fire any missiles today." Tal looked at Jackson. "We...um.. .ran into an issue. The test run was...postponed?" Tal looked toward Jackson, who gave him a small lopsided smile.

"We ran into some trouble," Jackson admitted, saving Tal from his daughter's interrogation. His smile faded and he sighed. "We found the missing freighter."

"The *Cerulean* something?" Maisy asked.

"The *Cerulean Sailing Star*," Tal confirmed.

Jackson nodded. "It was adrift in the asteroid belt we were going to use as target practice. Dumb luck. The area has been tapped out and abandoned for almost a year. No one should have been anywhere near it."

Maisy knew *adrift* was not a good word. "The crew...?"

"Dead," Jackson answered abruptly. "Cargo gone, of course."

While she considered and discarded multiple questions, Maisy remained silent for a moment. No matter the details, this had not been a fun mission for the crew of the *Sky*. Maisy glanced around the table at their faces, solemn and tense. "I'm sorry, guys."

Gray sighed and reached for the pitcher to start pouring water into glasses, passing them around the table. "Which park did you go to, Maisy?"

Maisy accepted the verbal baton gratefully. "The big one up on B deck. I scared the Cits by sitting on the grass," she smiled.

"I'm surprised they didn't call the CSS on you," Joe said, wagging his finger in Maisy's direction. She'd seen the Citadel Station Security harassing a couple of teenagers for using rollershoes on an upper deck. It seemed like overkill to have grown men with shocksticks run after a couple of kids having fun.

"There's no sign posted saying you can't sit on the grass. And it's artificial anyway." Maisy pointed out. "It's not like I could hurt it." Maisy considered the food on her plate and wondered out loud. "Are the other stations like this?"

"Like what?" Gray asked.

"So straight, so tight," Maisy floundered, reaching for the right word. "Do you know what I mean? No one here ever seems to really break the rules."

Joe laughed. "You've been hanging out with the wrong people!"

"Or the right people," Gray interjected.

Maisy shook her head. "I mean, like, important rules. People do small things and the CSS are right there to come down on them like a ton of bricks. But no one is robbing banks or stealing wristbands. Where's the crime?" The crew looked at each other for a moment, considering the question. "Or am I wrong? Do those things happen and we just don't hear about it?"

"Maybe a bit of both," Tal answered thoughtfully. "I suspect there is less crime here than on Earth simply because of the self-screening nature of interstellar travel. But I also think there are probably a lot of things that happen on the Citadel that we lowly peons never hear about."

Maisy's ears perked up, because Tal's thought process mirrored her own. "What kinds of things?"

"Well..." Tal hesitated, put on the spot. "Corporate espionage has seriously escalated recently and that's the kind of crime—and the kind of criminal—that wouldn't necessarily be deterred by the financial and logistical barriers of space travel." Warming to the topic, Tal leaned forward, his food forgotten before him. "Petty crime just isn't worth it out here. Either you've paid too much for your ticket to need to steal something like a wrist unit or you've been brought out here by the Citadel management to do a job, all of which pay enough to again preclude the need to commit petty crime. So what's left are the big ticket heists—which out here are corporate secrets—or the thrill criminals, who are just in it for the game."

Maisy nodded along with Tal's theorizing, but Jackson shook his head. "I don't know how much corporate espionage is going on. The screenings every arrival goes through are pretty intense."

"Then how are the raiders getting freighter itineraries? There's no way these are attacks of opportunity," Tal insisted. "Someone knew where the *Star* would be and intercepted her. And murdered twenty-seven innocent people in cold blood."

Silence descended over the table. Maisy hesitated, but in the end she couldn't help herself.

"Murdered?"

Tal ran a hand over his face and looked at Jackson for direction. His captain grimaced.

"Yeah, Maze," Jackson sighed. "The crew were shot, executed."

Gray looked down at the table and shook his head. Ann's face was pale. Joe pressed his lips together and set his food back on the plate in front of him, wiping his hands with his napkin.

Tal leaned his elbows onto the table and rested his forehead in his palms for a moment. Staring down at the table he said, "I've never seen anything like that." Gray laid a hand on Tal's shoulder, patting gently as he continued. "There was no struggle. No signs of a fight. They were just all lined up in a row in the cargo bay." Tal shuddered and Gray moved his hand across Tal's back to give him a one-armed hug. On his other side, Ann reached across Joe to put her hand on Tal's arm.

"At least we found them, kid," Jackson told him quietly. "I know it was hard to see that today, but the fact that we found them means that their families will have closure."

"I'm sorry." Maisy looked around the table. Ann gave her a sad smile and Jackson patted her on the arm. Tal took a deep breath and raised his head, giving Maisy a grateful nod. His eyes glistened but he was under control.

"We're going to head to a different sector tomorrow to test the missile upgrades, " Tal stated quietly.

"I'm sure they'll do great." With Maisy's encouragement, the tightness around Tal's eyes and mouth relaxed.

"Thanks," he said.

Jackson cleared his throat. "Not tomorrow," he said firmly. "The missile tests can wait until next rotation. Tomorrow we're staying on station and running some exercises."

"Exercises?" Gray asked, an eyebrow raised.

"Exercises," Jackson confirmed, a gleam in his eyes. He glanced over at Maisy and smiled. "Want to tag along?"

Maisy had no idea what said exercises might entail, but she honestly had nothing better to do.. "Absolutely."

Dinner was uneventful after that, punctuated by Joe's slightly off-color jokes, which earned him a punch on the arm from Ann. He was still rubbing the sore spot as they all shuffled from the dinner and made their way toward the residential halls. Maisy fell back behind Jackson and Ann as they discussed options for alternative training run locations. Tal moved into position at her side as the hallway narrowed.

"That was a pretty astute observation about the lack of petty crime on the station," Tal said.

Maisy looked up at him in surprise. "Thanks."

Tal nodded and they walked on in companionable silence. When they reached his turn, Tal peeled away from the group with a round of goodnights. At the next hallway Joe went one way and Gray the other. Jackson and Ann walked ahead of Maisy until they came to Ann's door.

"Goodnight, guys," Ann said as she slipped into her room.

Jackson and Maisy's door was at the end of the hall. Inside, Maisy went right up to her loft and changed into her tank and sweatpants that she slept in. As she poked her head around the partition Jackson had lowered the table in the living area and was sitting bent over his tablet. He'd raised the panel in the top of the table to use as a secondary screen and was scrolling through data while making occasional notes on the tab.

Maisy came halfway down the small staircase and sat on a step. She reached down to pull open the drawer carved into the step and took out her cleanser. Squirting a little into her hand she rubbed it over her face and into her hair, massaging her scalp. Her dad continued to work as Maisy rubbed a little more of the cleanser into her underarms before placing the bottle back into the drawer. Next she took out her toothbrush and bit down on the semi-circle mouthguard. The handle flashed green to signal the end of the cleansing cycle and Maisy set that back inside the drawer and slid it shut. Elbows on her knees she watched her dad working for a moment.

"You've had a long day, dad. Try not to stay up too late."

Jackson looked up and smiled, then glanced down at his tablet and sighed. "The tugs just arrived with the *Star*. I'm setting up the parameters for the scanners to collect samples and log findings. I've already had three threatening messages from three different Citatech reps demanding the ship be released for sanitation and recommission immediately." Jackson scowled and shook his head.

"Wow," Maisy replied. "That seems unusually callous, even for Cits."

"Joe's theory is that the corporations have factored the losses into their profit sheets already and the ROI on any defensive actions or investigations doesn't meet their thresholds."

"So they're just not going to do anything about it?" Maisy was somehow not surprised and thought Joe might actually have a point. His jaded paranoia when it came to the corporations was not unjustified.

"We're going to do something about it," Jackson said firmly. "The safety of the people out here is my responsibility."

"I know it means a lot to you," Maisy said softly, frowning.

Comprehension entered Jackson's eyes. "So do you, Maisy. And so did your mom. But they needed me," Jackson paused. "And you guys didn't."

Maisy swallowed hard and stood up to go back to her loft. Jackson jumped up quickly and grabbed her hand as she turned on the stairs.

He looked up at her earnestly. "I'm so sorry about your mom, Maze. But I'm so glad to have you here. To have had the chance to get to know you."

Maisy squeezed his hand back. "Me too."

3

Things fall apart

The handball ricocheted against the stark white wall of the court and nailed Tal in the back of the head. Maisy felt a flash of regret as she dived for the rebound. The synth-leather of the ball smacked against her hand and she twisted her body midair to send it flying toward Ann. The redhead caught the toss and redirected it to the blue square on the adjacent wall as Maisy's shoulder plowed into the deck.

Gray and Joe groaned as the buzzer signaled the end of the game and they limped over to Tal, helping him up off the floor. Ann bounced over to Maisy and offered her a hand, beaming.

"Thanks for the assist, Maze," she said brightly as she hauled Maisy to her feet.

"Anytime."

Jackson walked up and wrapped an arm around each of them, looking extraordinarily pleased with himself.

Gray stood with arms crossed, frowning in their direction.

"This feels like a setup," he grumbled.

Beside him, Tal rubbed the back of his head and nodded. Joe, bent over at the waist, hands on his thighs, waved at them all half-heartedly, still gasping for breath.

Jackson laughed at his friends.

"I'm sorry, are you blaming me for your mistake in underestimating my girls?" He gave Maisy and Ann each a squeeze before releasing them to bend down and retrieve the ball.

"Your girls, huh?" Gray scoffed, rolling his eyes.

Ann was smiling at Jackson, her face flushed with exertion. When she swung her eyes to Maisy there was a hint of trepidation and Maisy gave her a wide smile and a wink.

"He thinks we're girls," Maisy told her, shaking her head. Ann burst into giggles while Jackson held up his hands, apologizing profusely.

"You could have at least warned us," Gray complained.

"Quit your whining, man," Jackson taunted.

"Warned them?" Maisy asked. "About what?"

Jackson looked over at her as they lined up on the start line again, glee in his eyes. "That you're my kid."

Maisy just shook her head as he laughed at his own joke. She glanced at Ann and shrugged, but Ann was laughing too. The buzzer sounded for the beginning of the new round and Maisy rolled her eyes at them and focused back on the game.

Jackson spiked the ball into the center of the court, causing the circle in the floor to flash red and officially start play. Maisy leaped between Joe and Tal to grab the rebound. Gray's large form was between her and Ann so Maisy flung herself away from the other two men before launching the ball back toward her dad.

Gray was yelling commands to Tal and Joe, coordinating their movements around the court, but Maisy's team was silent. Ann passed her the ball over Tal, his head swinging to track its movement but his reactions too slow to intercept. Maisy looked for Jackson and found him before the goal, already waiting for her.

An hour later she and Ann were in the women's locker room, still celebrating their last win. Maisy stuffed her sweaty clothes into her bag while chuckling at Tal's expense.

"I swear I wasn't doing it on purpose!" she laughed. "It was as if the ball was just naturally attracted to his head." After the third time even she wasn't sure she believed it was an accident.

"Poor Tal," Ann shook her head in mock sorrow. "I'm sure his heart is broken." Seeing Maisy's raised eyebrows, Ann exclaimed, "You have to know he has a crush on you!"

"On me?" Maisy scoffed. "I hope you're kidding!" Maisy paused to face Ann as they approached the locker room door, her smile faltering. "You are kidding, right?"

Ann smiled and pushed past her out the door, the sound of the guys milling around the hallway ending the conversation.

As Maisy entered the atrium, she glanced up toward the top of the dome. It had been staged to look like natural light and she tried to imagine that it was the sun beating down on her. The temperature had increased gradually over the past weeks, supporting her fantasy. She'd mentioned the increase to her dad but he'd just shrugged.

Circling the open area to approach the entrance of the glide, Maisy stumbled to a halt. Sometime during the night the entire glide system had been removed. In its place was a set of tubes standing on the far side of the central shaft of the station. Maisy started walking again. As she got closer, it became apparent that these were old fashioned elevators, only big enough for one or two people to enter at a time. She joined a small crowd of people gathered around the elevator doors.

"Sue!" she said, recognizing her dad's neighbor standing with her young daughter, Joanie.

Sue's frown cleared as she saw Maisy. Little Joanie cried, "Maisy!" and dropped her mom's hand to give Maisy a hug.

As Maisy gave Joanie a squeeze she watched Sue press the panel beside one of the doors. The panel and her wrist unit flashed red. Sue stood there in confusion for a moment, and jumped when a man pushed in from behind her.

"Excuse me," the man said tersely. He wore black cover-alls and had a toolbelt around his waist and goggles hanging around his neck. He tapped on the panel and it flashed green. The door slid open and he slipped inside.

Sue stepped forward as if to hold the door, "Hey! How did you do that?"

"I've got a work order up on C deck," the man said. "Notice went out last night. No access to upper decks without a work order."

Maisy stepped forward, "No access?" But the door was closing and the only response was a whooshing sound as the elevator whisked the man up and away.

"What the hell?" Maisy said out loud.

"Language!" scolded Joanie.

Maisy ruffled her hair in apology.

"The bodega didn't get a delivery from hydroponics this morning," Sue told Maisy. "There's only frozen reconstituted protein substitute." They both made the same face. "I bet they have plenty of fresh food at the big market on B deck."

I bet they do, thought Maisy. For the hell of it she tried the panel and wasn't surprised when it flashed red for her as well.

"I know it's expensive," Sue said, almost to herself, "but I don't want Joanie just eating that processed crap."

Maisy hesitated, her mind racing, and asked, "How does the hydroponics delivery get to the bodega? They don't come down the glide, right?"

"No..." Sue drawled out. "I've seen them come through the back of the store. There's a whole system of halls back there and I guess they have their own glide. Or an elevator." She shrugged.

"Thanks!" Maisy replied. "Bye, Joanie!" she called as she spun around and walked quickly back the way she'd come. This felt like an important development. She tapped her wrist unit to initiate a call to her dad and watched as it spun and timed out. *The Sky must already be out on patrol*, Maisy thought.

The G deck bodega was positioned at the corner of the two main thoroughfares on this side of the deck. During the day, the walls were open on both sides, so Maisy slipped in and scanned the small store. As Sue had reported, the hydroponics cases, where fresh fruits and vegetables from the station labs were displayed for sale, were completely empty. The store manager was sitting on the floor in front of the cases with an autodriver in hand, removing the panels across the front.

Maisy sidled up to the man and asked casually, "No hydro today?"

"No," he replied shortly, not bothering to look at her.

"Do you expect a delivery tomorrow?" Maisy asked.

"No," he barked. "Not today, not tomorrow." The final screw came out of the panel he was working on and the man wrenched the panel away from the case and slammed it down beside him. Scooting himself in front of the next panel, the man began working on that one. He sighed and lowered his driver. "No more deliveries down here," he said, his anger draining away. He sat silently for a moment more then resumed his task.

Maisy stepped away, circling the shelves to the back of the store. The hatch to the storeroom stood open and Maisy slipped through without hesitation. A quick scan of the room revealed two doors, one to the left next to a window showing a standard office, and one to the rear. Maisy moved quickly to the second door, tapping the panel and hoping it wasn't user restricted from this side. The door slid open silently and Maisy stuck her head out, looking left and right. The door opened into a gray hallway that ended in what looked like an old fashioned freight elevator.

Ducking her head back into the storeroom, she grabbed a small box from one of the shelves and placed it in the door's track. She quickly ran down the hall to the elevator and tapped the panel. It flashed green and displayed a countdown to arrival for the car. This elevator wasn't restricted at least. The doors opened and Maisy stepped inside. She tapped the control panel for B deck and glanced at the still propped open storeroom door as the elevator hatch slid closed.

The car lurched and began moving upward. A second later the doors opened onto a similar hallway. This one had doors on both sides, spaced evenly. Maisy moved quickly down the hall. The old fashioned set of double doors at the end opened easily for her and she found herself in a refuse room, slightly bigger than the one near her dad's apartment.

This one had a series of larger than usual hatches, each one marked for organic, plastic, or metal refuse. At the opposite end of the room was another swinging door. Maisy pushed through to find herself at the end of the market hallway on B deck.

The market was much quieter than it would normally have been at this time of day. And Sue was right, there were plenty of fresh vegetables. Maisy walked up to one of the displays and pulled her mesh shopping bag from a side pocket of her backpack and shook it out. She filled her bag with an assortment of fruits and veggies, then grabbed another bag from a nearby rack and filled that up too. Moving to the end of the stand, she waited while the owner tallied her purchases and then waved her wrist unit at his reader.

"Quiet today," she said conversationally as the reader turned green.

"New rules," the man muttered, placing his reader back on the cart. "No more down station riffraff allowed on the upper decks. Not great for business but I can't say I'm sorry."

"Riffraff?" Maisy prompted.

"The coverall contingent. They're good at drinking their pay away, but not much else."

What a prince, Maisy thought, and walked away without another word. Deciding to test a theory, Maisy headed toward the atrium. There was no one waiting near the elevators on this level. Maisy tapped the panel and it immediately turned green and the door slid open. Inside her only option on the control panel was G deck. The panel was obviously reading her wrist unit and limiting her access. She selected G and the doors slid shut. A second later they opened again on her deck.

There were still a few people standing by the elevators and they gave her a funny look but no one asked and Maisy didn't volunteer. She walked purposefully past them and exited the atrium.

Two doors down from her dad's quarters, Maisy paused outside a hatch, tapping the panel. After a brief wait the door slid open and Sue stood there with a quizzical look on her face.

Maisy handed her one of the bags of hydroponics, waving to Joanie who sat behind her at the table. "I don't know when we'll get more," Maisy told her, "so make it last."

Sue took the bag mutely, her eyes widening in comprehension. Maisy turned to continue down the hall and Sue reached out to grab her hand. "Thank you!"

Maisy smiled, squeezed Sue's hand, and slipped away. Sue was still standing in her open doorway with a bemused smile as Maisy ducked into her dad's apartment.

Maisy jerked awake. She must have fallen asleep working on her tab. She'd been sitting upright with her back against the wall but now she was slumped over on her side, the tablet next to her on the bed.

A sound came from below. Glancing at the time, she walked to the top of the stairs. Jackson was hanging his jacket by the door, moving slowly.

Maisy came down and sat on her customary stair while her dad dropped onto the bench. "Go back to sleep, Maze," he said, his voice dull with exhaustion. "It's really late."

"Technically, it's really early," Maisy pointed out gently. "Do you know about the glides and the new restrictions?"

"Yes," her dad sighed. "There's a lot going on." He turned to look at her, his face just as tired as his voice. "We'll talk in the morning, okay?"

"Okay." Maisy hesitated for a moment and then continued down the stairs, moving around Jackson, who seemed too tired to function. She pulled out the bench to make her dad's bed, turned out the lights in the kitchen and took herself back upstairs. She heard Jackson hit the bed and nothing else.

Jackson

The lights in the unit automatically brightened at 0600 every morning. By 0630 they were set to full and Jackson was already done with the bathroom and starting breakfast when Maisy sat on her step to do her face and teeth. He once again marveled at the self-sufficient teenager he had inherited. He had always known Mary was a special woman and a great mom, but living with her daughter every day made his heart ache sometimes.

Jackson reached into the cooler to grab water, then hesitated. "Hey, Maze. When did you hit the market?" he asked curiously.

"Yesterday," Maisy replied, putting her autobrush back in its drawer. "It's kind of a long story, actually."

Having sat through several unpleasant meetings on the subject the day before, Jackson nodded. "I bet." He flipped his bed back into the bench position and pulled down the table top. Grabbing two bananas from the cooler, Jackson slid onto the bench and gestured Maisy over to the table. "Enlighten me."

Rolling the other bench to the table, Maisy accepted the offered banana and carefully removed the peel as she described encountering Sue in the atrium the previous day and the shock of the missing glides and canceled deliveries. Jackson nodded along, not surprised by this part of the story.

"It turns out," Maisy said with wide eyes, "that there are old fashioned freight elevators that service the commercial units."

"Yes, there are," Jackson drawled. "But those are only accessible through the commercial units. By employees of the commercial units."

"They may also be accessible by people who wander through the open doors of the back rooms of said commercial units," Maisy postulated, raising her eyebrows and widening her eyes.

"Oh, is that right?" Jackson was pretty sure he should be mad.

"On a completely unrelated note," Maisy added, "Sue has enough veggies to get her through a week or so, but we'll need a new plan by then."

Jackson sighed and dropped his forehead into his hand. Considering his options, he settled on "discretion is the better part of valor." Grabbing Maisy's peel and his own, Jackson retreated into the kitchen. When he returned, Maisy had righted all of the furniture and was waiting by the door. He grabbed his bag and met her eyes.

"Please keep your head down today. The situation on station is in flux and tempers are high. We'll get through this and figure out a path forward, but for now, just don't get into trouble. Okay?"

Maisy nodded. "Okay."

Her dad reached forward and gently pulled her head to him to plant a quick kiss on her forehead.

"I'll see you later, Maze."

Jackson ducked out of the unit and walked quickly down the hall, lost in his thoughts. Now that the three former marine corvette teams were officially part of Citatech Security Services, as the senior officer Jackson reported to the head of Citadel Security, Tindell Burt. Before the buyout, Jackson had limited contact with Burt but he'd known he didn't like the man. Now that he'd spent more time with him, he knew why.

There were three kinds of marines. Those who got in and got out and went back to their normal lives and never looked back. Those like Jackson who were all in. They might leave the service for one reason or another—as he considered doing after Maisy was born—but they were always marines, to the core. Once they wore the uniform it became imprinted on their identity.

Then there were those who joined the service to hone their skills and then sold those skills to the highest bidder. To put it simply, Burt was a mercenary.

Jackson strode into the beta dock to find the *Sky* already fueled and prepped for launch. Entering the hatch he hit the intercom embedded in the wall. "All hands on board?"

Joe's voice came back, "Everyone but you, boss."

Jackson released the call button and hit the hatch panel. The door slid shut and the panel flashed green. Making his way to the bridge, he found his crew all at stations. Observing them for a moment, Jackson sighed.

"Well, we're a chipper bunch this morning, aren't we?" He took his seat, pulling a canister of coffee from the bag he placed at his feet. As he pulled the tab he turned it toward the red dot on the lid and the can heated the liquid. Taking a cautious sip, Jackson waited for the caffeine to hit his system.

It was going to be a long day of patrol, but at least he wouldn't have to deal with the likes of Burt.

"Ann, do we have our alternate test site loaded into the flight plan?"

The redhead turned and gave him a tired smile. "Yup, we're ready to go."

"Alright, team, let's get out of here."

4

Sky to the rescue

Jackson

Jackson clapped Tal on the shoulder. "Great job today, kid. The numbers on these new Citatech munitions are excellent."

"Too excellent," Tal muttered, not looking up from his console. "When the data doesn't fit expected parameters that means we missed something somewhere. Or we had bad data..."

Jackson patted Tal on the shoulder. "Don't stress too much about it, kid. At least the error was in our favor."

Tal sat back from the console and turned to look at his captain. "But next time it may not be. These numbers were not within the margin of error. It means there's a problem somewhere and I need to figure it out because next time it might bite us in the butt."

"Oh, kid," Jackson sighed. "There are so many things waiting to bite us in the butt right now. It's going to have to take a number." Jackson patted Tal on the shoulder again and headed back to his command chair in the center of the bridge. Pulling forward the comp built into the armrest, Jackson scanned through Tal's data, frowning. The kid was right that something was off about the new ammunition, but Jackson suspected he knew the culprit.

The new missiles weren't the standard s-marine issue. They were Citatech Corp rounds and the specs they'd received had been from Citatech. The warheads didn't match the advertised Citatech munitions. On a gut feeling, Jackson pulled up the specs for the SN warheads of the same caliber and shot those over to Tal's console.

"Hey, Tal. Run your model with these specs and see if our field test results match those projections." Jackson folded his screen away and pulled up the main plot to the big screen. "How long until station, Ann?"

"Just over an hour, Captain," Ann replied.

Jackson nodded and pulled up the report he had started on his comp. He was making progress when Tal appeared at his elbow. Jackson looked over and smiled at the young engineer's expression. "Numbers right on, huh?"

"The specs you sent are for the new 9th generation Suki-Nyberg warheads, aren't they?" Tal asked with a frown.

"They are indeed." Jackson drawled. "What is your conclusion based on the evidence, Corporal?"

Tal twisted his lips. "My conclusion is that the warheads provided to us by Citatech are the product of corporate espionage, sir."

"I concur with your assessment." Jackson stated baldly. "The question is, what are we going to do about it? There is no higher authority to report this data to. Not anymore."

Tal ran his hands through his thick hair, not improving it. "I didn't sign up for this, Jackson."

"None of us did, kid." Jackson placed a firm hand on Tal's shoulder. "We'll figure out a plan of action. Tomorrow. For today, let's get the *Sky* home and get some rest, okay?"

Tal nodded. Jackson gave his shoulder one more squeeze and released the younger man, who turned and went back to his station. Jackson turned toward the weapons station and met Gray's concerned gaze. Next he glanced at Joe, who frowned, his eyes jaded. Ann had her head down and frowned at her console.

"Hey, Joe. Do you see this?" Ann tapped her console and a data stream lit up the main bridge display. Joe tapped his panel and held a hand to his earpiece as he listened. Making more changes, Joe listened again, his face serious.

Turning to Jackson, Joe said, "We've got a distress signal." Tapping his console, Joe sent the audio to the overhead speakers and the room was flooded with static, beneath which a human voice began to take shape. "...is the *Oro Zapato II*, repeat, we are under...," the voice faded again under the static. Joe made more adjustments on his console. "...Need assistance. We are entering the Simon Belt, two light minutes from the primary base..." The signal faded again but Jackson had heard enough.

"Ann, get us there."

"Yes, sir."

The pilot ran her hand across her panel to disengage their in-system thrusters and activate the *Sky*'s jump drive. Making adjustments to their course and velocity, Ann prepared the ship to jump to the outer perimeter of the belt. "Initiating emergency jump in...five...four...three...two...one...jump."

Jackson's stomach lagged a second behind them during jumps, but it had been many, many years since he'd shown any visible sign of the brief spike of nausea that accompanied interstellar travel. His stomach settled back in place as the stars assumed their positions around them. The plot on the main screen updated and identified their new position.

At his console, Joe was listening intently. "Got it," he said.

Suddenly a voice cut through the small bridge. "Mayday, repeat, we are under attack. This is the *Oro Zapato II* on route from Gamma 367. We are under attack by an unidentified ship. Our engines have been disabled."

Tal swiped a new plot from his console to the left secondary screen. "Ann, they're here." Ann fired up their intersystem thrusters and headed for the heat source Tal had identified.

As they neared the system, the signature resolved into two separate ships. The freighter on the left screen fit the information he'd unearthed for the *Oro*. It was a huge vessel, easily ten times the size of the *Star* but composed mostly of cargo space. The system added data to the board it became available, including crew, cargo capabilities, engine, and mass.

By comparison, the *Oro*'s attackers were a gnat attacking a bear. The attacking ship's profile was being built on the right hand secondary display. It wasn't much bigger than the *Sky*, but it was bristling with weaponry. This one was all engine and guns.

The computer couldn't identify the ship, but Jackson knew what it was. It was a pirate ship, purpose built to attack much larger vessels, run them to ground and overwhelm their defenses in a short amount of time.

The screens continued to update as they got closer to the ships and Tal pointed out key capabilities as he identified them. On the left screen, the data was also starting to include the damage being done to the *Oro*—and it was bad.

The huge ship had obviously turned and ran when the raiders had popped up on their sensors and their aft section had taken the brunt of the hits. Like most heavy freighters, the cargo was located at the bow and the engines basically pushed from behind. Where smaller ships like the *Sky* had a single in-system engine and separate jump drive, a freighter would have a series of dual engines that worked in parallel and distributed their load. It also made for a target rich environment for any pursuers.

As the detail in the rendering on the screen continued to build, the back end of the *Oro* had been eaten away by its attackers and looked like nothing so much as a block of cheese that had been nibbled on by giant mice.

It was hard not to make the comparison, but Jackson knew that damage likely signified lives lost. There were compartments open to space and large gouges near the engines that represented internal explosions. And he knew that the crew of the *Oro* was well aware of the fate that awaited them if the raiders caught them. Rumors had already been flying fast and free even before the *Star*'s discovery. Freighters in the quadrant would have all been briefed on what happened to her crew.

Joe was monitoring the distress call over his ear piece and suddenly he sat up straighter. He turned his head to meet Jackson's gaze, his hand held to his ear piece, listening intently. Joe's face blanched and he tapped his panel to switch the audio back to the bridge speakers. The same voice as before was still speaking, but their tone had taken on a desperate edge.

"...Say again, this is the *Oro Zapato II* and we are under attack. If anyone is receiving this transmission, we need assistance. We are a family ship, with twelve children on board. I repeat, we have twelve children on board. Mayday, mayday..."

"Shit." Jackson said softly. The vast majority of big freighters like this were owned, or at least leased by, the corporations. Family ships had been more common twenty years ago, when distances meant months or even years between ports. With recent advancements—especially the ability to jump much more precisely and therefore much closer to planets—voyages were a lot shorter and family ships had become less common. Leaving your spouse and kids behind when you'd be gone for two weeks was a lot easier than being gone for two years.

"Open a channel to them," Jackson told Joe. "Ann, adjust our course to intercept the unknown contact."

Joe tapped at his console. "Channel open."

"This is the...*CSSS Windless Sky*, responding to your hail," Jackson stumbled over the unfamiliar call letters. They had been the *UCS Windless Sky* until recently, a United Coalition Ship. Now their call sign was Citatech Security Services Ship, which just didn't sound right. "Hang on, *Oro*. We are moving to intercept your pursuers."

"Oh my god, thank you!" The captain's voice was thick with tears. Behind him, a chorus of voices cried out in relief. "We've lost three of our engines and two members of our crew, including our first mate, my son." The captain's voice broke off in a sob and the voices around him rose and fell.

Jackson and the crew of the *Sky* listened as the man choked back his grief and carried on. "We're redlining the remaining engines to maintain our distance but we can't hold it much longer."

"We've got you *Oro*," Jackson told them. Glancing at the plot's real time intercept countdown and calculating their firing range, he continued, "Hang on for another...twenty-one minutes."

"I honestly don't know if we can."

Tal leaned toward Jackson to get his attention and whispered urgently, "If the *Oro* turns toward us it would give the raider room to close but it would cut our intercept time." Jackson nodded, thinking fast.

"*Oro*," Jackson said, tapping out calculations on his comp. "Can you change course thirty-seven degrees starboard, eleven degrees down. That will cut down our intercept time to...fourteen minutes?"

"We'll lose some of our distance, but yes, we can do it. Executing now."

Jackson nodded to Ann and she made the appropriate changes to the *Sky*'s trajectory. The plot on the main screen updated the intercept time as the *Sky* changed course. Across the vastness of space, the great freighter began turning, slowly. The time to intercept scrolled down even faster.

Tal leaned toward Jackson. "If they turned a few more degrees port, it would cut down the intercept time even further," he said quietly.

Jackson mirrored his lean. "Yeah, but then the hull of the *Oro* would be between us and the raider's corvette. We wouldn't be able to get a clean shot while they continued to chew up her back end." Tal nodded and grimaced, moving back to his station.

Jackson sat back in his chair, eyes moving between the intercept time and the *Oro*'s damage report. Now that they had changed their angle, there was less surface area available to their sensors but the trail of debris being left by the big ship told its own tale.

Jackson glanced over at Gray and found him prepping plots on the weapons console. Gray looked up. "Ready?" Jackson asked.

"You know I am," Gray replied. Jackson nodded and smiled. He and Gray had been in worse situations and he knew Gray had already planned out multiple scenarios to cover the next hour. He had a plan, a backup plan, and a backup plan to the backup plan.

Speaking of backup plans... "Joe, zip up the audio file and all of the data we've collected so far and launch a drone toward station, please."

"You got it, Captain," Joe replied.

A moment later Jackson felt the deck vibrate as Joe launched a drone from the *Sky*'s belly. The drone was the size of an old fashioned beach ball. Its plasticor hull was practically invisible and its cold fusion thrusters didn't leave enough of a signature to register on any but the most sensitive equipment—and only then at ultra-close range. The little drone raced away from the asteroid belt and hurtled towards the Citadel. It didn't have jump capability but its acceleration would continue to build until it entered the station's range and uploaded its payload. Then it would flip and take the long way around to return to the station.

"Jackson, I'm sending you a timecode and coordinates to send to the *Oro*," Gray said a second before a file pinged on Jackson's console.

"Got it," Jackson replied as he opened the file. "Looks good," he said. "We'll be able to release two salvos before the raiders can even see us." Jackson hesitated for a moment before continuing, "Of course, the *Oro*'s pilot will need a clean change of underwear."

"At this point they probably already do," Gray pointed out with a rueful grin.

"True," said Jackson with an answering smile. "Let's do it." Jackson opened a secure line to the *Oro* and deployed the instructions on a tight beam that the raiders wouldn't be able to intercept. Sending the file this way meant that any eavesdropper had to literally be placed directly between the two ships to intercept their communications.

"Joe, reopen the channel." After a moment of static, the *Oro* captain answered. "*Oro*, I just tightstreamed a file to you. Once you confirm receipt and compliance we will go to radio silence." Seconds ticked by and then the captain of the *Oro* came back on the line.

"*Sky*, we have received your file." There was still some background noise on the bridge of the other ship but the mood had definitely calmed since they'd received the *Sky*'s response to their distress signal.

It was now quiet enough that the sound of other captain swallowing echoed through the bridge. "We understand, *Sky*. And we will comply. Thank you."

The transmission cut off and the *Sky*'s bridge was once again silent.

"Tal, prepare to route all emergency power to the forward shields," Jackson said calmly. "Ann, I'm forwarding the file we just sent to the *Oro*. You'll need to make course adjustments at the timecode."

Jackson turned toward Joe and Gray. "Gray, send the munitions inventory for your first two salvoes to Joe. Joe, we're going to need self-destruct codes ready for those rounds in case the *Oro* doesn't change trajectory in time. I need you to calculate the last possible second we can send the codes." Joe's console pinged before Jackson finished talking and Joe was looking at Gray's figures, an eyebrow raised.

"We're going to deliberately fire at the ship we're trying to save? Awesome." Joe said, deadpan. "I'll have the self-destruct codes ready in two minutes. It'll take me a little longer to calculate the point of no return numbers. They'll be different for each round and I'll have to recalculate for any course corrections on either end."

"Is it faster if you just determine the earliest trigger point for each salvo?"

Joe thought for a second, "Yes, if I identify the farthest round in each array, that shouldn't change."

"Okay, let's go with that," Jackson nodded.

Each member of the *Sky* crew was heads down, working on their data, when the display of the smaller ship updated.

"Check out the ID on the raider ship!" Tal blurted out to the bridge at large. Everyone's eyes flew to the right side secondary screen, where the computer had thrown up a preliminary ID for the previously unknown ship. *The SNCS Penny Farthing* was a brand new commissioned corvette of the Suki-Nyberg corp navy, less than six months old. The system had been able to identify her based on the rarity of her hull configuration. This was a brand new body type and size for SN corvettes and there were only a handful flying at the moment. The AI had used registered flight plans to narrow down the possibilities to one.

Jackson's mind began to race. The pirates were *Suki-Nyberg*. So were the...

"Can we change the default self-destruct codes on the missiles?"

Tal and Joe shared a panicked look.

Tal tapped at his screen, sliding data over to Joe's console. The two of them pored over the info, keeping one eye on the countdown to the *Oro*'s course change ticking over on the main screen.

"Here!" Tal cried, tagging a file and sending it to Joe, Gray, and Jackson. "Gray, can you update the bios at this line?"

Gray was hunched over his console, fingers flying. "Joe, I'm adding the letter Z to the end of every round's ID. You'll need to recompile your codes but I think this will work."

Jackson looked through the data and took a deep breath. "If the raiders have the codes, we have to change them. If the new codes don't work, though, we're depending on the *Oro* to have the ability and will to execute her maneuver in less than five minutes."

Gray nodded without looking up from his screen, his fingers flying. Jackson sent a brief prayer out into the universe and sat back in his command chair, trusting his crew and the *Oro*'s crew to do their jobs.

"Okay!" Gray hit the last key and executed his changes. They all held their breath for a moment until the faint ding of the comp's confirmation rang out. Gray glanced at the ticker on the main board and the ones he'd anchored to the corner of his panel. "Firing first salvo in ten seconds. Captain, are we cleared to go?"

"Yes, cleared to go!" Jackson replied without hesitation.

Gray started his countdown. "Firing in five...four...three...two...one...first salvo has been launched."

Rows of green indicators lit up his panel and the deck of the *Sky* shuddered as dozens of high intensity rounds launched from the ship. Jackson glanced at the clock. One minute until the next salvo was away. He used the time to double check his crew's work. If the change didn't replicate through the rounds it meant that the SN crew might destroy their missiles in the air. If the change went through but the new self-destruct codes weren't properly compiled it meant that if the *Oro* failed to turn, they risked blowing up the ship they were trying to save. Given they could no longer track the damage that the *Penny* was doing to the Oro's engines, that was a very real possibility. Jackson confirmed the last calculation and shut the tab. There was nothing more they could do at this point.

"Second salvo firing in five...four...three...two...one...second salvo away." Again faint vibrations shook the deck as Gray's board lit up green. He sent the datastreams from the first salvo to the main bridge display.

On the screen, the larger components of the asteroid field and the three ships in the system were joined by the two clusters of red dots winging their way across the space between the ships. The ticker on the screen scrolled to zero and the *Oro* swung out of position and away from the two smaller ships. The smaller ship behind them continued on their course for a moment before adjusting their trajectory as well, but it was already too late. Hidden from their view by the *Oro*'s bulk were dozens of warheads, seconds from impact.

Gray had done an excellent job of predicting the *Penny*'s course. If the captain of the raider ship had responded more quickly to the *Oro*'s course change, they might have dodged the bulk of the salvo. If the *Penny* had detected the salvo and the captain had belayed the order to follow the *Oro*, he might have been able to let the salvo pass harmlessly between them before continuing his pursuit. But instead the Captain had taken crucial seconds to recognize the *Oro*'s course correction and then had no time to take evasive action when the missile battery was suddenly revealed.

Jackson watched the board begin lighting up with hits and damage reports. The majority of Gray's rounds made contact and as they closed with the raider ship it floundered under the attack. Damage reports glowed on the board as the *Sky*'s missiles made contact.

As the crew of the *Sky* waited for their second attack to hit the raiders, they held their breath as one. Although both ships were technically in the same class, corvettes, it was obvious that the new ship far outclassed the *Sky* in pure firepower.

"Damn," Jackson said quietly, watching the *Penny* angle away from their second salvo.

Gray grimaced and did some quick calculations on his console. "Impact prediction just dropped to seventeen percent"

There were tense faces across the bridge of the *Sky*. The other captain had turned quickly enough to thwart their second attack. The *Sky* had maxed out the amount of rounds they could throw at one time and minimized the time needed for reloading, but there had still been enough of a window to give the *Penny*'s captain time to react.

Now it was time to fight.

5

Maisy's afternoon

Maisy submitted her last assignment of the day and tossed her tablet onto the bed, flopping back onto her pillows. It was almost noon. Staring at the blank ceiling, she considered her options.

It had grown unpleasantly warm on G deck and she really wanted to head up to the big park on B deck, but she took her dad's warning seriously. There was something going on here and the last thing she wanted to do was cause problems for him.

Rising from her bed, Maisy slipped her tablet into her backpack and headed down to the kitchen area. Standing at the small counter she woofed down a banana from the cooler and headed out the door. Although she'd been on station a couple of months, she still didn't know many people besides her dad's crew and their immediate neighbors. All of her classes were remote, although she knew there was an in-person school on the upper decks for the children of the station management team.

Even on Earth Maisy had attended remote classes. There weren't enough kids in their rural county taking advanced courses to hold them in person. She remembered attending the local elementary school when she was little, but once she'd tested out of all the basic courses, there hadn't been much point. It had been lonely at times, but she and her mom had had fun. The courses available on the station network weren't quite as interesting as the ones she'd had access to on Earth, but the technical subjects were keeping her busy.

Sue's door opened as Maisy was passing by and Joanie stuck her head out, doing a double take when she saw Maisy.

"Maze!" the little girl cried. "Can you help me?"

Maisy smiled at Joanie, who was dressed in a bright pink coverall. "Sure, kid. What's up?" Maisy knew Sue was likely at her shift at the loading docks. Usually Joanie went to the creche on deck D when Sue had day shift.

"I'm not a *kid*, Maze. I'm eight years old now, you know." Joanie said with a well-developed sense of importance.

"I know! Your birthday cake was delicious." Maisy smiled even wider. Sue was an excellent cook and it was important to her that Joanie ate as many healthy, home-cooked meals as possible. Maisy had been the lucky beneficiary of Sue's cooking on multiple occasions. She knew her own mother would have shared Sue's horror at the standard fare aboard the station.

"It was *spectacular!*" Joanie announced. "I have some brownies my mom left for me. Do you want one?" Joanie stepped back and Maisy followed her into their unit.

"I would definitely eat a brownie," Maisy answered as she swung her bag onto a bench cluttered with pretty pillows. Sue and Joanie's unit was the same layout as Maisy and Jackson's but Sue had decorated it in bright, sunny swaths of fabric and Joanie's artwork hung from multiple surfaces. Sitting on the small kitchen counter was a plate of square cut brownies, topped in powdered sugar.

"Oh, man," Maisy sighed.

Joanie carefully folded a recycled paper napkin and lovingly placed a brownie in the center before presenting it to Maisy with the serious air of a sommelier.

"These have *real* chocolate with *real* avocados and *real* figs," Joanie announced.

Maisy accepted the brownie with the reverence it deserved and carefully took a small bite. The edge was crisp and the inside was gooey. It melted in her mouth and the chocolate flavor burst against her tongue. It was unbelievably creamy and just the right amount of sweetness.

"Joanie, your mom is a genius!" Maisy said as she went in for her second bite.

"Yes, I know," the little girl replied.

"So why aren't you at creche, kid?" Maisy asked between decadent tiny bites.

"We couldn't get there," Joanie told her, forehead creased. "They took the glides away."

Maisy swallowed her bite of brownie hard.

"I forgot about that," she said. "Did your mom try to call them?"

"I don't know. She was really unhappy. She said to just stay here and do my assignments on my tablet today like I would at the creche. I was doing that but now it's not working."

"The tablet?" Maisy asked.

"The tablet works, but I can't get the assignments." Joanie explained. "Can you fix it?" Joanie fished the tablet from a pile of pillows on the bench and passed it to Maisy.

"Let me take a look." Maisy licked the last of the chocolate from her fingers before accepting the tablet. She nudged aside a couple of pillows to make herself a place to sit. Joanie was right and the tablet itself seemed to be working fine. Entering the EDU module, the main list wasn't loading. Switching to Joanie's assigned courses had the same result.

"That's weird," Maisy said, thinking. Pulling her own tablet from her bag, she went through the same process...and watched the list spin. "It was working fine earlier."

"Yeah," Joanie agreed. "It was fine and then it just stopped working. I tried to call my mom but I couldn't get her. I was going to come knock on your door but then I saw you."

"Good timing." Maisy gave her a distracted smile as she tried several different methods of connecting to the EDU module. Going out to a browser, Maisy accessed the general station subnet and received a security prompt she'd never seen before. Her wrist unit flashed red and the browser window announced *access denied* in bold letters.

"Well, this isn't good," she mumbled to herself.

"If it means I don't have to do lessons anymore, it can't be *that* bad," Joanie replied.

Maisy swallowed a laugh. "I'm not sure how your mom would feel about that." Smile fading, Maisy clicked through her apps. Anything requiring net access was offline. The wifi was up but her account was blocked. Going back to Joanie's tablet, Maisy found the same thing. The net was still there, but they didn't have access to it.

Knowing her dad was off station and that he wouldn't answer, Maisy messaged him, *Hey*. The little circle next to the message stayed hollow and gray. It would turn solid gray when sent, dark gray when received, and green when read. Maisy stared at the little gray circle. Nothing.

"I'm going to go head down to the bodega and see if their system is up," Maisy told Joanie. "I'll stop by later and let you know what I find out, okay?"

Joanie frowned. "I don't want to stay here alone anymore. It was different when I was doing school stuff, 'cause I knew I could call my mom if I wanted," she said. "Now it feels creepy."

Maisy thought for a second. The kid was right. It did feel kind of creepy. But she also didn't want to give Sue a heart attack if she came home and Joanie was gone.

"Let's leave your mom a note, okay?" Using Joanie's tablet, Maisy let Sue know that the net was down and Joanie didn't want to stay in the room alone so she'd be with Maisy. She told Sue they would go to the bodega and then head back next door. Maisy set the tablet to wake on motion and propped it up on the table, where Sue would see it as soon as she walked through the door.

"Okay," Maisy told Joanie, grabbing her bag from the bench and swinging it over her shoulder. "Let's see what we can see."

The girl preceded Maisy out the door, skipping carelessly down the hall. Apparently any anxiety she'd been feeling had passed.

Maisy smiled and shook her head. Her own worries were not so easily quieted.

Joanie knew the way to the only food shop on their deck by heart and led the way. Maisy followed behind, her mind racing. As they moved toward the center of the station, the hallways got wider and more crowded. People were milling about aimlessly. Maisy overheard snippets of conversation and realized the net access issue was widespread. People were meeting in the corridors to discuss the issue and sounded increasingly frantic. As they passed by the open windows of the Big Tow, there were people at every table, all speaking and waving their arms.

As they approached the bodega, just short of the main atrium, the small store was overflowing with people. It looked like most of them were getting off of their shifts and still dressed in their work station coveralls. It was crowded enough that Maisy reached for Joanie's hand and the little girl grasped hers in visible relief.

They pushed through the crowd to the side of the store and made their way inside. The hydroponic stands were completely gone but the manager didn't seem any happier. His store was full of people who didn't seem to be buying anything.

Grabbing a milky drink from a cooler along the wall, Maisy weaved in and out of the people talking, dodging some wild gesticulations, to make it to the counter. The man seemed prepared to yell at her for approaching him but sighed gustily when she placed the drink on the counter. Maisy made eye contact and shrugged apologetically as the manager picked up the bottle and held it to the scanner embedded in the counter in front of him. The screen displayed the price and she waved her wrist unit over the scanner. The cuff blinked green once, so at least that was working.

When the confirmation of the payment flashed on the screen the manager handed the drink back to Maisy.

"Thanks." Maisy slipped the drink into her bag. "Looks like a party."

Twisting his lips, the man shook his head. "Not a party. Maybe a wake."

"What do you mean?" Maisy asked, even more alarmed.

"They're mourning the death of their freedom," the manager said quietly, "and they don't even know it yet."

"Because the net is down?" Maisy was genuinely confused. This seemed like more of a technical glitch than a political statement.

"The net is still there, girl," he told her. Normally Maisy would have strenuously objected to the appellation but at this point she didn't want to interrupt his flow. "The net's still there, you've just lost access to it."

"Permanently?" Maisy clarified, her heartbeat accelerating.

The old man nodded. "Who here can fight the corporation? Who can question their decisions? The coalition government has thrown us to the wolves, mark my words."

He sounds like Joe, Maisy thought. All of Joe's rants about indentured servitude. The paranoia must be contagious. As bad as the corporations could be, the conspiracy theories surrounding the withdrawal of the coalition government from the rim quadrants already had tinges of hysteria. This mess was going to drive them over the cliff.

"Thanks." Maisy pulled Joanie away. In the short time they'd been talking with the man at the counter, the store had become even more crowded. Maisy held firmly to Joanie's hand as they worked their way out of the store and back to the main hallway. People were everywhere, standing with tablets in hand, tapping in frustration.

Finally the two of them made it back to the residential hallways. They stopped at Joanie's door and it opened in response to her wrist unit.

Maisy stuck her head in. "Sue?" she called out, but there was only silence. Everything was as they'd left it.

"Okay, kid," Maisy looked down and gave Joanie a reassuring smile. "Want to come hang out with me for a while?"

"Yes!" Joanie replied without hesitation, making Maisy laugh.

"Okay, then!" Maisy ruffled Joanie's hair and gestured for her to lead the way down the hall to Jackson's unit. Her wrist unit flashed green and the door slid open. Inside was just as she'd left it and she wondered what she'd do to keep an eight-year-old occupied for what could be several hours.

"Would you like to read one of my books?" Maisy asked.

"Would you read it to me?" Joanie countered.

Maisy smiled. "Sure. Grab a bench, I'll be right back." Maisy hopped up the stairs to her loft and grabbed the worn paperback sitting on the small table beside her bed. Back downstairs, Maisy moved the right-side bench to make an L-shaped seating area.

"See, it's like a real reading nook," Maisy told Joanie, who was fascinated by the book Maisy had produced.

"This is a real book," Joanie said, ignoring her. "It has real book smell." Joanie breathed in the book and Maisy tried to hide her smile. Her mom would have loved Joanie. *A bookworm in the making.* Maisy's smile faded and she swallowed hard. Forcing a lightness into her voice, Maisy asked, "Why don't you give it a try? It's been a long time since someone read to me..."

Joanie took the bait and curled up on the bench with the book, opening it up to a random page. "*Because I could not stop for death, he kindly stopped for me.*" Joanie glanced up, concerned. "Uh oh." Looking back down at the page, she continued. "*The carriage held but just ourselves and immortality.*" Joanie looked up at Maisy. "A carriage is like an autocar, right? I've seen those in vids."

"But not in real life?" Maisy asked. "Were you born on the station?"

"Yup! But mom says she'll take me to visit Earth one day. She's looking for a contract that will take us off the station."

"She is?" Maisy encouraged her.

"She said the stations aren't going to be safe anymore, especially for kids, so it's time to go back to home system."

Maisy wanted to dismiss Sue's concerns the same way she'd seen her dad treat Joe's paranoid rants, but at this point they were starting to ring true. Things were changing and the fact that their lives were completely at the mercy of Citatech seemed like a Very Bad Thing.

After delivering her second-hand proclamation of doom, Joanie went back to her reading with the carelessness of youth. "*We slowly drove. He knew no haste.*" Joanie hesitated.

"Do you know what haste means?" Maisy asked.

"It's the opposite of slowly, right? So fast. But he's not fast."

"Right!"

"And this is the guy in the long robe with the big curved ax thing, right?"

"Right!" Maisy laughed. The door panel chimed and she climbed from the bench to tap the panel. The door slid open to reveal a harried Sue on the threshold. Her eyes darted past Maisy and when they landed on Joanie the relief that washed over her looked like a physical wave. Sue sagged in the doorway, breathing deeply.

"I'm so sorry, Sue! I left a note on Joanie's tablet. When the network went d—" Maisy's explanation was cut off as Sue pulled her into a hug. Joanie ran up and joined in. Maisy stood still for a moment, before awkwardly patting at the mother and daughter who were invading her personal bubble.

"Thank you, Maze," Sue said as she pulled away, a hand brushing over her forehead. "You did exactly the right thing."

Joanie transferred her hug from Maisy to her mom and Sue wrapped an arm around her daughter. Her face had lost its haunted look but Sue still looked exhausted and ready to crash.

"Come sit down." Maisy moved back from the doorway. Sue followed her into the small room, Joanie attached to her hip. Sue sank gratefully onto the bench with Joanie by her side and Maisy perched on the other leg of the reading nook they'd made.

"What's going on?" Maisy asked bluntly.

Sue shook her head slowly as she gathered her thoughts. "A transport arrived today, full of new CSS soldiers."

"Marines?"

"No, not marines. Not like your dad. These are mercenaries. Soldiers for hire." Sue continued. "You know about the glides and the restricted access. This is more of the same. The corporation is tightening its grip on the people here." Sue hesitated. "Have you noticed it's getting hotter?"

Maisy frowned at the non sequitur, but nodded.

Sue sighed. "The Citadel is powered by the reactor that runs the ore processing plant at the center of the asteroid. When this rock was mined out, they dropped the power plant into it and built the station above it. The output of the plant has always been limited by the heat it bleeds off into the station. There's a huge temp difference from the top decks, that are exposed to space, compared with the lower decks that are closer to the plant and insulated from the big cold out there."

Sue jumped up from the bench and began pacing in the small space. "When this place was built, the coalition set the operating standards. The living areas had to be kept between eighteen and twenty-four degrees, that meant that the plant couldn't run at full power. To add insult to injury, Citatech had to use power to heat the upper levels to keep them warm enough. Now that the coalition government has pulled out, those rules are out the window. Or at least, aren't going to be enforced. So the station manager is raising the output of the plant to keep the outer decks at the optimal temperature without spending energy to heat them. This is great for Citatech's bottom line—but it means we're going to roast down here." Sue looked at Maisy, her face serious. "This is just the beginning."

"You mean it's going to get hotter?" Maisy asked, in disbelief.

"A lot hotter. I think this is why they've cut network access. So that we don't have any way to complain or organize a protest. We don't have any way to tell anyone what's going on here."

Joanie huddled into Sue's side. Maisy knew she probably didn't understand exactly what Sue was saying, but she knew her mom was upset. She knew her mom was *scared*.

"Do you guys want to stay for dinner? My dad should be home soon and we can brainstorm some ideas," Maisy offered.

Sue reached out and squeezed her hand. "Thank you, Maisy, but we're going to head home. And thank you again for keeping Joanie company this afternoon." Sue forced a smile.

"I was bribed with a brownie," Maisy said seriously. This time Sue's smile was genuine and she seemed much calmer as she and Joanie walked to the door. Maisy watched them turn into their unit and then stepped back inside, letting the door slide shut behind her.

Stepping into the kitchen area, Maisy opened the cooler and considered her options. Grabbing a banana, she put off deciding about dinner and headed up to her loft to read while she waited for her dad to come home.

6

Dogfight

Jackson

"Okay, team. Looks like we're going into this old school." Jackson sighed and clapped his hands. "Ann, set an intercept course. Tal, set up a new ticker on the *Oro*'s board. I want a countdown to the point when they're completely clear and the raider won't be able to catch up with their velocity."

"Yes, sir," Tal responded. A few moments later he slid the the countdown to the *Oro*'s display on the secondary screen. "There you go, Captain."

"Ladies and Gentlemen, that is our goal," Jackson gestured to the new ticker. "We need to keep these assholes busy for the next twenty-four minutes so that the men, women, and *twelve* children aboard the *Oro* make it safely out of here." Jackson glanced around the bridge of the *Sky*. There was determination on every face.

Ann looked up from her station, the plot updated on the center screen. "We'll close to effective weapon's range in three minutes, Jackson, assuming they don't turn to meet us."

Jackson nodded. "Oh, they're going to turn. We're not going to give them a choice. Right, Gray?"

"Damn straight, Captain!" Gray responded firmly and a chorus of voices joined his. This crew wasn't taking no for an answer.

Gray continued, "I've got sixteen of the big XRs spooled up and ready to go. If I use the 5B net pattern they'll have no choice but to swerve or flip."

"They'll flip, trying not to lose ground on the *Oro*. We have to make them fight." Jackson knew that the more the *Penny* maneuvered, the more time the *Oro* would be able to pull away from her. "Ann, as soon as Gray fires his missiles, push down and starboard. Let's see if we can get in some shots behind their forward shield and encourage them to move insystem at the same time."

"Yes, sir."

"Tal, once we change trajectory and angle our nose away from the *Penny* be prepared to reduce power to front shields and funnel everything you've got into the aft thrusters. They'll be bleeding acceleration so let's do what we can to match their velocity."

"Yes, sir," Tal replied and nodded toward the secondary screen displaying the *Penny*'s stats. "Damage reports coming in. Looks like we took out at least one compartment but their engines are still at full capacity."

Jackson bit back another curse. *It had been a long shot anyway*, he acknowledged to himself. The other ship would try to shoo them off like a gnat. It was the job of the crew of the *Sky* to bite them in the ass for it.

"Approaching weapons range," Ann announced, her voice tight but even.

"Gray, you're cleared to fire when in range," Jackson said calmly.

Gray had already prepped the salvo on his console, but he tapped through each missile's settings, double checking the updated codes and making minute adjustments as the clock counted down and the ships converged. "Firing in...five...four...three...two...one. Missiles launched." Ann executed her course change and the *Sky*'s thrusters fired.

"Any fluctuations in the *Penny*'s engines?" Gray glanced over at the young engineer, who was watching his own console intently.

"Not ye—Yes! There it is! She's flipping!" Tal pointed at the secondary screen showing that the position of the *Penny Farthing* had flipped over and her acceleration was falling rapidly. In response to the threat of Gray's salvo the captain of the *Penny* was protecting his ship by inverting her and placing his heavy main shields toward the *Sky*. That meant that they didn't have a shot at the *Penny*'s engines, but it also meant that those engines were now pointed the wrong way. The *Penny* was now losing ground on the *Oro* quickly—as the bigger ship sped toward the edge of the system where it would be safe for her to engage her jump drives and flee to safety.

"They've launched missiles," Tal reported. "They're too far out to do much damage. Should I launch ECM?"

"Do it," Jackson told him.

Jackson glanced at the *Oro*'s data on the board, noting that she was less than ten minutes from jump. On the main screen the *Sky* and the *Penny Farthing* were no longer on the same plane. The *Sky* had turned down and right in relationship to the other ship's path. Instead of aiming directly at them in a head-on collision, they were now set to pass them, the *Penny* on their left and slightly above their line of flight. That put them in perfect firing position.

"They're coming up fast, Gray. Let's try to send them home limping. Fire at will!"

"Yes, sir!" Gray readied his shots and fired. He used the saved formations he'd built into the system, able to engage dozens of rounds with a single click. The computer assisted in the finetuning of each shot, taking advantage of the *Penny*'s profile in the databanks.

"Damage reports coming in," Tal said, making no attempt to hide the excitement in his voice. "There's definitely atmosphere leaking from at least two compartments."

The bridge lights flashed red and an alarm cut through the deck.

"Proximity alarm!" Ann cried.

The inertia generators lagged as the *Sky* lurched violently to port. Ann scrambled to pull the *Sky* into a tight turn as the main screen lit up with multiple close objects directly in their path. From the starboard side of the ship, the sound of a blast rumbled faintly and the deck shuddered.

"Tal, report!" Jackson demanded. "What the hell did we hit?"

"It looks like a piece of the *Oro*! It must have broken off as they turned. We've got a breach near engineering." Tal scrolled through the incoming damage report. "Shields are damaged! Down to forty-three percent! Twenty-seven percent! We're losing them!" Tal frantically cycled through each circuit trying to reroute the shields to a stable conduit.

"Gray, do we still have weapons?" Jackson asked.

"Yes, sir!"

"Throw everything you have at them. Tal and Joe, haul ass down to engineering and get our shields back up. *Now!*"

The two men unhooked their harnesses and leapt from their stations. Tal hit the hatch a second before Joe and then they were running flat out down the corridor. On the bridge, Gray was methodically spooling up every round in the *Sky*-'s bay in a staggered formation. They flew from the *Sky*'s weapons ports in continuous waves.

"Their second salvo is coming our way, Jackson," Gray said calmly. "This one is going to be a lot harder to miss."

"Acknowledged. Launch ECM. Ann, take evasive action. Pattern 1A." Jackson leaned forward in his command chair. They were approaching the *Penny* fast. The next couple of minutes would bring them to their closest point. This was the best opportunity for either side to get in a good shot and they needed those shields.

Jackson created an open channel to engineering. "Tal, Joe? Give me some good news, guys."

For a moment there was just static, then Tal responded, out of breath, "The engine compartment is on fire. The breach is contained but the suppression system was damaged. We're working on it!" He realized the background noise was the roaring of flames.

Jackson pulled up the damage reports on his panel and watched as the shields completely failed. Another alarm sounded in response and he cut it immediately.

Over the open comm line, the sound of the two men battling the blaze in engineering echoed. The sudden whoosh of the suppression system filled the bridge for several seconds. In its wake, the silence was broken only by panting.

"Fire's out," came Tal's harried voice over the comm. "Manually rerouting shields over the life support system."

More alerts popped up on Jackson's panel, showing small areas of hull damage where their ECM had engaged the *Penny*'s missiles a little too close for comfort.

"Jackson, we've got more rounds coming our way," Gray said from his station. Jackson glanced at the main screen. Several dozen markers popped up in the ever closing distance between the two ships. Gray's missiles rained down on the raiders but the salvo headed their way was a flood.

"Crap," said Jackson. "ETA?"

"Two minutes, fifteen seconds," was Gray's calm response.

"Tal? Joe? Did you guys hear that? You've got about two minutes to get us some shields."

"Yes, sir," came Tal's response. The two men were working frantically to manually reroute the shield's circuits. He knew they were likely tearing out big chunks of the life support system, but they could deal with that if they survived the next two minutes.

"We've almost got it, Jackson," Tal said, his voice strained as if he were stuck under a panel, which he likely was. The shields popped back up on Jackson's console and he tapped at the control to re-engage, holding his breath. The light stayed red for a moment and flipped to green, showing eighty-three percent.

"You did it, boys! Get back up here!" Jackson crowed. A second later, the bridge of the *Sky* lurched sideways as an explosion rocked the ship and the *Sky* shuddered. Aftershocks kept the bridge moving and Jackson struggled to focus on the data streaming into his panel.

"Direct hit!" Gray called from his station.

Jackson gripped his console as the bridge stabilized. "Engines," he said. As he watched, the temperature of the *Sky*'s reactor entered the red zone. The bridge lights turned red and an alarm pealed. "Shit. It's going to blow." Jackson brought his hand down on the big red button that had appeared on his console. A distinctive tone sounded throughout the ship that every marine, merchant, or sailor of any kind was familiar with. *Abandon ship.*

Jackson unhooked his harness and looked toward Gray and Ann. "Time to go."

Ann lunged up from her seat and ran for the hatch. Gray was frantically keying commands into his panel and Jackson put a firm hand on his shoulder.

"Now," Jackson said firmly, pulling the larger man from his station.

"Tal? Joe? Can you guys hear me? Head for the emergency pods. Reactor meltdown is imminent. Time to go, guys." Jackson hustled Gray through the hatch and followed Ann down the hall.

"Acknowledged, Jackson," came Tal's response and Jackson let out his breath. The emergency pods were situated below engineering and Tal and Joe would be there before them. The deck jolted as pods one and two launched from the ship a moment later, as he and Gray caught up with Ann going down the ladder to deck one. Ann stepped out onto the metal decking and looked up through the hatch at Gray, who was coming down the ladder.

"Go, Ann!" Jackson yelled. "Don't wait for us!" Ann turned away and took a step towards the compartment that housed the emergency pods. A rolling thunder shook the ship and kept building.

Heat blew through the hall, followed by a deafening blast.

Jackson glanced behind him to see a fireball consuming the corridor.

His eyes closed and he saw Maisy's face.

7

Bad news all around

Maisy's eyes snapped open and she knew before she looked at her wrist unit that it was already morning. Rolling onto her back, she couldn't believe she'd fallen asleep waiting for her dad, but she wasn't surprised he'd let her sleep.

Quickly changing her clothes, she started down her small staircase to the main area of the apartment and stopped. Everything was as she'd left it, the bench still pushed against the wall. Either her dad had been and gone—or he'd never come home last night.

Continuing down the stairs, Maisy sat on her customary step and pulled out her cleanser and toothbrush. It was definitely warmer this morning and she was already covered in a fine sheen of sweat.

Moving to the kitchen, Maisy realized she was starving. Pulling milk from the cooler, she poured herself a bowl of cereal and grabbed her tablet. She ate while cycling through her apps and sites to see if anything had changed since the previous day.

The answer was no. Maisy had no access to any of the EDU modules and couldn't log into the station net at all. It looked like she could send and receive messages, at least.

Creating a new thread, Maisy selected Jackson's name and typed out a brief message.

Did you come home last night? Anything you need to tell me?

Closing the window, she opened a thread to Ann.

Jackson didn't come home last night. Don't suppose you know anything about that?

Maisy chuckled to herself, hoping the red-haired pilot got lucky last night, but knowing that was highly unlikely.

Finishing her cereal, Maisy washed her bowl and spoon and put them away. Slipping the tablet into her bag, Maisy headed out the door. Since she couldn't get any info from the net, it was time to hit the streets, so to speak.

As she got closer to the wider hallways toward the center of the station, Maisy encountered more and more people and a low rumble of unhappiness. There was a general sense of disquiet, with occasional raised voices. The inhabitants of G deck were definitely beginning to understand their value in the eyes of the corporation.

The heat was not helping. No one seemed comfortable and tempers were short. As she neared the small park near the Big Tow, Maisy passed two men in coveralls arguing. One man pushed the other so that he rocked back on his feet. Regaining his balance, the second man gut-punched his companion and the hallway burst into chaos.

From nowhere, two uniformed CSS officers grabbed the two men. One black-helmeted officer used a shockstick to grab the punch-thrower around the throat and pull him backwards. The other grabbed the still doubled-over victim firmly by the arm. Within seconds all four were gone.

Maisy ducked into the Big Tow, looking for any familiar faces. Recognizing one of the marines from the crew of the second station corvette, Maisy approached her table.

"Hi, Stace. Have you seen Jackson this morning?" Maisy stopped abruptly at the look on the pilot's face. "What happened?"

"No one's talked to you?" Stacey asked, looking sick.

"No. What's going on?" Maisy asked again, taking a seat at the table.

"Maybe you should talk to—"

"Nope," Maisy interrupted her. "I'm talking to you. Tell me what you know," she said firmly.

"I don't know a lot. The *Sky* went to the aid of a freighter in distress and hasn't reported back in. The freighter was being run to ground by pirates but they made it back okay. All shot to hell and they lost some crew."

"And the *Sky?*"

"No one knows. We're heading out in an hour to her last known coordinates to search."

Maisy took a deep breath. "Will you let me know what you find? Or don't find. Communications are spotty. Come find me and tell me, okay?"

"Yes, Maze. I promise."

Without another word, Maisy left the Tow and continued through the station to the Atrium. Her mind racing, she eyed the new elevators and turned back. Going down the main hall, she approached the bodega and slipped inside. It was once again teeming with people, none of whom seemed to be actually buying anything. The manager looked extremely unhappy.

Suddenly a display went crashing over and canisters of tea went flying through the air. The manager came tearing into the crowd and a group of CSS officers pushed their way inside, their featureless black helmets gleaming in the overhead lights.

"This business is closed. Exit the premises immediately," one of them announced, as they pushed the customers out. Their helmets were completely opaque and it was impossible to tell which one was speaking, but the crowd began pouring from the store. Maisy ducked out, narrowly dodging the security shutters as they slid down over each open wall segment.

The men and women forced from the store were standing outside, facing the officers who had taken up posts along the two exterior walls. The two sides faced off, tensions high.

Keeping her head low, Maisy moved quickly away from the store and back toward her apartment.

As she rounded the corner the noise behind her hit a crescendo. She looked back to see a full blown riot had broken out. CSS officers were tazing people with shocksticks; punches were being thrown. There were too many people in the hallways and nowhere to go. Maisy was jostled as people tried to move away from the conflict.

She dodged panicked men and women, most wearing the distinctive black coveralls of station staff. Maisy's immediate goal was to get out of the public spaces. She swerved to avoid a boy with white blond hair as another group of CSS agents pushed through the crowds from the opposite direction. One of the officers pushed the much shorter boy out of the way and he wobbled. Acting on instinct, Maisy grabbed him as he lost his footing, holding onto him as he regained his balance.

They stood frozen as the group went by. As the last officer disappeared into the crowd in the direction of the bodega, the boy darted into the gap they'd left in the crowd moving away from the chaos. Maisy followed him and in moments the hallways were quieter as people moved with purpose toward their units.

The boy glanced over at Maisy, then down at his feet. He looked a few years older than Joanie. "Thanks," he said, glancing up at her face shyly. "That was scary."

"No problem," Maisy forced a small smile. "Time to get out of the hallways, yeah?"

"I'm not sure where to go," he answered, slowing down.

"What do you mean?" Maisy matched his speed.

"I used to live on E deck but my mom had an accident and they kicked us out of our unit."

Maisy stumbled to a halt. "What do you mean? Where's your mom now?"

"I don't know," he said, stopping and leaning against the white plasticor wall. People moved past them as they huddled against the side of the corridor. "We got separated and now my wrist unit won't connect to anything. We used to visit the bodega on this deck so I came down here, but then the new elevator wouldn't let me go back up again."

"You can come with me, okay?" Maisy started walking again and the boy followed. "We need to get somewhere safe. Then we'll figure out how to find your mom."

"Okay," he replied. "My name's Leo."

"Nice to meet you, Leo." She smiled, looking back at him over her shoulder. "I'm Maisy."

They rounded another corner and Maisy led Leo deeper into the residential hallways of G deck. When they finally reached her dad's unit, Maisy sighed in relief. There was no one moving in this hallway and everything seemed normal and quiet. She tapped the panel and waited for the door to slide open, but instead her wrist unit flashed red.

Maisy tried the panel again, but again the door stayed stubbornly closed.

"This is what happened to our unit," Leo said quietly. Maisy clenched her jaw and took a deep breath. Turning back, she walked to Sue and Joanie's door and tapped their panel. A moment later the door slid open to reveal Sue standing at the doorway, looking worried.

"Maze!" echoed down from the loft area and Joanie came hurtling down the stairs. The little girl ducked past her mom and grabbed Maisy in a hug. Over Joanie's head, Maisy met the fear in Sue's eyes.

"Can we come in?" Maisy asked. Sue looked past Maisy to see Leo standing behind her. She hesitated for a moment and then sighed and stepped back silently, waving them in.

Sue's tiny unit was intended for one person, max two. With four people taking up all of the floor space it became claustrophobic. Maisy realized her heart was pounding and sat on one of the benches, letting her backpack fall from her shoulder to the bench beside her as Joanie snuggled into her side.

"I'm sorry, Sue. My wrist unit won't open my dad's door. A fight broke out at the bodega and I met Leo in the hallway. He got separated from his mom and couldn't call her."

"It's okay, Maisy. We don't have access either. I'm not sure what's going on and I've been afraid to go out. If you guys can stay with Joanie, I'll go see if I can find out what's going on."

Maisy nodded, flanked by the two kids. Sue looked at the three of them.

"Why don't you guys make some lunch while I'm gone. Maisy is in charge, okay?" Sue leaned down to kiss Joanie on the head. "Be good, please. I'll be right back." With that, Sue slipped out the door.

"Move your bench over here, Leo," Maisy said as she lowered the table top. Once they had the seats arranged around the table, she led the procession into the tiny kitchen to raid the cooler. "How about cereal?"

A chorus of semi-enthusiastic responses greeted the suggestion, so Maisy grabbed the supplies and joined the two kids at the table.

Watching the kids dig in, a flash of anxiety washed over her and Maisy fought the urge to pull out her tablet and check the network for the millionth time or run back to her dad's door and try the panel again.

The definition of insanity, she thought, *is trying the same thing over and over again and expecting a different outcome.*

Maisy accepted that the door wasn't going to work. She had to try something different. She made herself eat her cereal, forcing down one bite at a time.

Joanie and Leo followed her lead and the three of them sat in silence, eating their cereal. Leo finished quickly and sat staring at the box of cereal sitting in the center of the table.

Taking the hint, Maisy asked, "Would you like another bowl?"

"Yes, please," Leo answered quickly, reaching for the box.

"When did you last see your mom?" Maisy asked, watching Leo scarf down his second bowl of cereal.

Leo shrugged, swallowing. "I don't know." He glanced up at Maisy, then looked back down again quickly. "It's been a couple of days, I guess."

"Where have you been sleeping?" Maisy asked.

"I slept in the bathrooms in the commercial district on E deck," Leo confessed.

Joanie's eyes went wide. "You slept in a bathroom?" she exclaimed. "Gross!"

"It wasn't that bad!" he countered. "It had a door that locked and it seemed pretty clean." Leo sighed and looked down again. "I didn't know what else to do."

The boy sounded tired and confused. "Where is the last place you saw your mom?" Maisy asked.

"We were at the citizen resource center on E deck when the big fire happened," he started.

"There was a fire?" Maisy asked, her mouth falling open as she stared at Leo in shock.

"Yeah. Everyone was yelling and pushing and they were closing the doors and trying to get people to leave and all the sudden there was a fire in the kiosk in the middle of the hallway. Everyone started running and I didn't see my mom. People were moving and they moved me with them. By the time I was able to stop, I was almost back to the atrium. I tried to get back to the resource center but everything was blocked by the black helmet guys."

"Your mom was trying to get help with your unit at the resource center?"

"Yeah, but they said they don't do that anymore. And I guess they don't do anything anymore. I went back a while later and there was a sign up saying that it was permanently closed."

"I can't believe there was a fire and this is the first I've heard of it." Maisy thought for a moment. "But I guess that makes sense. No one seems to have access to the net or communications. How would we find out?" she wondered.

"My mom said that a fire is the most dangerous thing that can happen on a station," Joanie pointed out.

"Your mom is right." *And that's why there are so many safeguards against it.* Before Maisy could follow that train of thought, the door to the unit pinged and slid open. Sue hurried inside, her face strained. She looked relieved to see her tiny apartment full of random children.

Rounding the table, Sue pulled Joanie into a hug while the little girl protested. Over Joanie's head, Sue met Maisy's eyes, trying to communicate something she didn't want to say in front of the children.

"Hey, sweetie," Sue said to Joanie, "Have you shown Leo your big tablet yet? Why don't you take him upstairs and play him some of the songs you downloaded?"

Joanie jumped up immediately, tugging Leo along in her wake. Sue sat in Joanie's abandoned seat and began absently closing the cereal box and consolidating the remains of their impromptu lunch.

Maisy was eager to hear what Sue had found out but she forced herself to be patient. The older woman needed a moment to organize her thoughts.

After a few minutes of fussing with the dishes on the table, Sue sighed and sat back in her seat. Above them the children played an upbeat dance song.

"Things are bad, Maisy," Sue said quietly. "The corporation is off the leash. No more coalition government to enforce the rules."

"What does that mean?" Maisy asked. "What rules are they breaking?"

"Pretty much all of them." Sue looked like she'd aged ten years in the last day. "This isn't just about management raising the output of the reactor and cooking the rest of us. Things are much worse than that."

"Worse than *that*? How?" Maisy asked. "I know they've cut our access to the net. And comms. Leo said there was a fire on E deck the other day that no one knows about. What else is going on?"

"A fire?" Sue said, a hand over her mouth. After a moment she shook her head and took a deep breath before starting again. "CSS is taking people. No one seems to know where. There's no due process, no protections." Sue frowned down at the table top. "It isn't safe, Maze."

Sue reached for her bag and pulled out her tablet. Tapping through the options, she tried several different permutations before laying the tablet on the table in frustration. "I'm going to see if I can get tickets on the next transport to Earth. I can't do anything on the net, so I'm going to have to go to the office down by the bay and see if I can buy tickets directly."

Sue stood up again and moved back to the door. "Will you stay here until I get back?" Maisy nodded. Sue glanced up at the loft, indecision on her face. "If Joanie comes down before I get back, tell her I'll be quick, okay?" Maisy nodded again, a lump in her throat as Sue slipped out the door.

Music echoed down from the loft but the main level of the unit was silent. Maisy didn't want Sue and Joanie to leave the station, but she understood Sue's concerns. She was right. The Citadel wasn't safe.

A week or two after Maisy arrived on station, she'd had dinner at the Big Tow with her dad's crew and Ann had been asking about her life on Earth. Jackson had told her about the farm and Ann mentioned that she had also grown up in a rural area, which was apparently unusual for people who ended up on the stations.

"People who grow up under the big sky tend to get claustrophobic up here," Ann had told her. "Folks from the big city never learn to look up and they don't miss it."

"Why did you leave Earth?" Maisy asked. As much out of legitimate curiosity as to avoid being psychoanalyzed at the dinner table herself.

"The marines put me through flight school," Ann beamed. "Now I've got the biggest sky to fly in. Nothing but stars in every direction." With her red hair and bright smile, Ann seemed to glow with happiness in the gutted belly of the old space tug turned diner. Jackson sat next to her, looking relaxed and happy.

"So you're in it for the long haul?" Maisy prompted.

"That wasn't the original plan," Ann admitted. "I was think-ing I'd take my pilot's license and go back to Earth and take a commercial job. But things change, and..." Ann hesitated. "I'm happy here." She shrugged and looked down. Ann's eyes moved to Jackson's hand, resting on the table beside her. Oblivious, Jackson stared at her downbent head, smiling.

"That's really nice." Maisy's gaze searched the two of them. She was caught off guard when Tal picked up the line of questioning.

"This has to be really different for you then, Maisy," he threw out. "What do you think so far?"

Maisy worked hard to keep from frowning at him. "It's fine. Ann's right that it's really similar to life in the city. Everything is owned by the corporations."

"That's definitely true," Tal nodded. "But there are a lot of different options out here, even if they are all somehow connected to the corp."

"I can't really see myself working for Citatech. I'll stay until I finish my baccalaureate. After that, we'll see." Tal's face fell. She glanced at Jackson, who was also now frowning. Beside her, Gray nudged her elbow and Maisy looked up at him.

"Your dad really loves having you here. He'd definitely miss you if you were gone," the big man said, smiling kindly.

Maisy returned his smile. She'd discovered Gray was pretty much always kind, which was ironic since his job was literally to blow things up.

"I'm sure he'll be happy to get his bedroom back at some point," Maisy joked, sparking laughter around the table. After that, the conversation had moved on.

It had only been a couple of months, and staying on station long enough to finish her degree no longer seemed like a viable option—even before she was kicked out of the EDU apps. At this point, she wasn't sure she'd last another week.

She wasn't sure that any of them would.

8

Into the depths

Maisy didn't notice when the music from the loft stopped. She was lost in thought when Joanie and Leo came bouncing down the stairs. Pushing her concerns and the nagging worry about her dad to the back of her mind, Maisy glanced at her wrist unit. She was shocked to see how late it was. Sue had been gone much longer than Maisy thought she'd be.

"Hey, guys," she said to the kids bopping down the stairs. Maisy made an effort to be upbeat in front of Joanie and Leo. There was no point in worrying them.

"Are you ready for some dinner?" Receiving enthusiastic responses, Maisy walked into the small kitchen to look at their options. "Do you have something specific in mind, Joanie?" Maisy opened the cooler and peeked inside.

"Do you have hotdogs?" Leo asked.

Ew, Maisy thought.

"Yes!" Joanie replied. "Let's have hotdogs, Maze!"

Maisy sighed and shook her head and pulled three hotdogs from the depths of the cooler, mildly shocked that Sue kept such things on hand. As she prepared the food, Maisy asked the kids about the music they'd been playing in the loft and then listened gratefully as Joanie carried the conversation with a long, involved explanation of the evolution of her favorite boy band.

Sitting at the table and choking down her highly processed, tube-shaped meat substitute, Maisy let the chatter wash over her. Sue should have been back hours ago. Her first instinct was to go out and find her but Maisy knew she couldn't leave Joanie and Leo and she definitely didn't want to take them out into the station during the dark hours. Especially given the violence she'd seen earlier.

No, the important thing right now was to keep the kids calm and get them settled in for the night.

Once they'd finished dinner, Maisy made a game out of setting up a bed on the floor for Leo. They raided Sue's linens and cannibalized the pretty pillows from the bench and Leo ended up with a comfortable little nest at the foot of the stairs. Maisy used the rest of the linens and pillows to set up a bed on the bench for herself.

"Joanie, bathroom and then up to bed. Okay?" Maisy was pleasantly surprised when Joanie didn't argue. Once she was done Maisy waved Leo toward the bathroom. Then it was her turn.

Evening prep done as well as it could be, under the circumstances, Maisy stood for a moment and gazed at her reflection in the small mirror above the sink.

For a moment, she allowed herself to remember the pretty yellow walls of her bathroom at home. She'd loved the black and white checkerboard floor and the white subway tiles, the real porcelain sink and big framed mirror. In the summers, the morning sun would pour in, bouncing off the bright walls. Her mom would stick her head in to check on her progress. She'd be halfway through her own morning routine, her curly mass of hair held back from her face by a headband, massaging her favorite cream into her face.

Maisy remembered kissing her mother's cheek in the mornings and teasing her because her face cream had left a sharp, medicinal smell.

She didn't allow herself to think about where Jackson was at the moment. Right now, she was responsible for two kids who needed their moms. Once Sue got back, she'd have the tickets for her and Joanie to get off of the station. Then Maisy could focus on finding Leo's mom. Once the kids were safe and where they needed to be, she'd worry about Jackson. And herself.

Back in the main living space, Maisy sent Joanie up to the loft and got Leo settled in his little nest. Both kids had been under a ton of stress and were ready to crash. Maisy settled onto the bench and took out her tablet. Once again she cycled through all of her apps and tried every way she could think of to get onto the net. Nothing.

Setting the tablet aside, she lowered the lights in the room and leaned back against the pillows.

Several hours later, Maisy opened her eyes to find the room still dark. The lights automatically lightened at the station's "dawn," so she knew without checking her wrist unit that it was early. Leo slept in his nest of pillows and blankets on the floor, just the top of his tousled blond head visible. There were no sounds from the loft. Maisy picked up her tablet and scrolled through her apps—again—with the same results.

No connection, no communications.

Silently swinging her legs over the side of the bench, she stood and made her way to the bathroom. She scrubbed her teeth with her finger, making a face at herself in the mirror. At this point she wasn't surprised that Sue hadn't returned. She realized in the back of her mind she had been half expecting it. The question was how long should she wait before taking the children from the safety of the unit to go look for her.

There were two factors to consider. Maisy had taken an informal inventory of the food in the unit the previous night and knew that they couldn't stay hidden away for more than a couple of days. But even more importantly, she knew that the feeling of safety here was completely false.

Embracing her sense of resolve, Maisy left the bathroom and entered the kitchen, raising the unit's lights to fifty percent. Not trying too hard to be quiet, she began pulling out breakfast options. There were some very nice meat-substitute sausages and the remainder of the hydroponic fruits. She set the fruit on the table, noting that Leo was beginning to stir. Carefully stepping over the boy, Maisy walked up to the loft.

Joanie was flopped out across her bed, limbs akimbo and blanket hanging off the bed onto the floor. Maisy sat on the edge of the bed and poked at her shoulder gently with one finger.

"Hey, kiddo." When that didn't elicit a response, she poked a little more firmly. Finally, Maisy put her hand around Joanie's shoulder and shook. "Joanie, wake up," she said sternly. Finally the girl's eyes fluttered.

"Good morning! Please get dressed and come downstairs and we'll have some breakfast, okay?"

Joanie blinked silently at Maisy, who sighed. Maisy was either awake or asleep. She tried to be sympathetic to the morning grogginess that most other people seemed to suffer, but she didn't understand it.

Changing tactics, Maisy retreated back to the kitchen. Leo was now sitting up and rubbing his eyes. Maisy arranged the sausage onto a plate and put it in the cooker. Within seconds, the smell of the meat-substitute, which was objectively much better than its taste, began permeating the small living space. Above her head there was movement and Maisy smiled.

"Whatcha makin'?" asked a quiet voice at Maisy's elbow, causing her to jump. Leo still seemed half awake so Maisy sent him to the bathroom with instructions to make an effort to clean up.

By the time Maisy and Leo were sitting down at the table, Joanie had magically appeared from above, surprisingly alert.

The three of them dug in, attacking the food in silence. As their eating slowed, Joanie put down her utensils and folded her hands on the table before her. Looking seriously at Maisy, she asked, "My mom didn't come back, did she?"

"No," Maisy said. "We're going to have to go find her."

Joanie nodded. "Ok. We'll find her." The little girl set her chin and squared her shoulders.

Maisy gave in to her instincts and drew Joanie into a hug. Suddenly Leo was there too and Maisy lifted her arm and Leo ducked into the hug. Maisy held her eyes wide and looked up at the ceiling for a moment, her throat burning and her heart pounding.

Pulling back from the children, Maisy took a deep breath and said, "We've got this, right?"

"Right!" they echoed, with far more confidence that Maisy felt.

"Let's finish breakfast and then we'll find your moms." The kids wolfed down the rest of their food in record time.

"Joanie, does your mom have a place she keeps special documents or important things?" Maisy asked. Sue had expected to come back here, but who knew if any of them would return at this point. They couldn't assume they'd have the chance to come back. Maisy tried not to think of the book of poems her mother had given her, sitting in the loft of the unit she could no longer access. She'd brought so few things with her from her old life.

Losing one old book shouldn't hurt so much, but it did.

Joanie had pulled out one of the drawers built into the loft stairs and placed it on the table. Inside were two thumb drives and a credit chip. Maisy took the three small items and placed them in a zippered pocket on the front of her bag. Moving back to the kitchen, she grabbed the protein bars she'd noticed before in the cabinet and dumped those into her bag as well.

"Is there anything else your mom would want to have if she weren't coming back here?" Maisy didn't want to shake Joanie's confidence, but if there was anything Sue needed from this unit, it made sense to take it with them.

"I don't think so," Joanie answered.

Maisy nodded, swinging her bag onto her shoulder. Both of the kids had their wrist units and nothing else. "Stay close to me, okay? It's really important that we all stay together." Joanie and Leo nodded seriously. "If we get separated, we'll meet at the bodega. Got it?"

"Got it!" They said in unison. Joanie was at least two years younger than Leo but almost as tall.

"You guys are really doing great. Let's go find your moms!"

Maisy led the procession out of the unit. *Three orphans into the storm*, she thought to herself then immediately pushed the idea away.

They tried Maisy's door again then carried on down the deserted hallway. As they ventured into the wider corridors, the hallways remained empty and the only sound was the eery echo of their footsteps.

Approaching the commercial district, Maisy hesitated. A new sound rumbled up ahead. As they got closer it became the din of a crowd, punctuated by a few shouting voices.

Motioning to Joanie and Leo to stay behind her, Maisy peeked around the corner into the main hallway lined with shops. There was a crowd gathered around the Big Tow, with smaller groupings scattered through the area. People were all talking, some loudly. Maisy searched for any familiar faces but recognized no one.

Grabbing the two kids by the hands, she started around the corner, sticking to the wall and edging around the crowds. Listening hard, she caught snippets of conversations.

"They took him off the schedule and now no one knows where he is..."

"...then CSS just burst into the room..."

"H deck is completely deserted. They sent Paul down there to cap the recyclers last night..."

Pulling the kids into the alcove of a closed shop, Maisy strained to hear the last conversation. *How could an entire deck be empty? Where did the people go?*

"My neighbor just got moved up to D. He said they're consolidating the living quarters so they can increase output on the processor. They'll flood the lower decks and use them as insulation to dissipate the heat."

"Geez, could they break any more regulations? There's no way that would pass a safety inspection."

"Well, they just canned the last inspector. No one cares anymore. There are no rules."

Drifting further down the hall, the two speakers moved out of Maisy's hearing. Sweeping the crowd for familiar faces, she continued moving the kids along the edge of the corridor. She didn't expect to find Sue at the transport office, but it would be good to know if she'd made it there yesterday.

As they passed the Big Tow, a group of CSS officers approached from the opposite direction. Once again, Maisy dragged the kids into the shadow of a closed storefront, watching quietly as the CSS passed, eight officers walking abreast across the hallway with shocksticks in hand.

Suddenly the screen on Maisy's wrist unit turned red. Releasing Joanie's hand, Maisy tapped on her unit but the thing had bricked. Through the corridor voices rang out in surprise. Glancing around, there were dots of red light throughout the crowds.

"Maisy," a little voice whispered next to her. Joanie was tugging on her shirt, her own wrist unit red. Leo was having the same issue.

Crap, Maisy thought. *There's no way this is a good thing.* She pulled the kids deeper into the shadows of the alcove, pulling Leo's arm across her body and reaching for Joanie's other hand. Maisy turned to shield their wrist units as the CSS passed behind her, threading their way through the crowd.

Maisy stood frozen, looking over her shoulder as the officers began pulling the men and women with red units from the crowd and lining them up along the opposite wall. Quietly, Maisy moved the kids down the corridor, away from the crowd. She was relieved to see the Bodega open.

She slipped inside with the children and moved toward the back. There were only a handful of people at this end of the corridor and the shop seemed empty. Standing behind a shelf, Maisy dropped the children's hands and worked to get her wrist unit off. Placing it on a shelf, she reached down to remove Joanie and Leo's as well. She shoved all three units behind a box of freeze-dried noodles and glanced up as the manager came out from the back room.

"You shouldn't be in here," he said.

"Why not?" Maisy asked. "The communicators don't work and we can't get on the net. What's going on?"

The shopkeeper looked taken aback, either by her confrontational tone or by the fact that she didn't know what was going on.

"The CSS is sweeping up anyone who isn't pulling their weight and they're going to be deported," he told her finally.

"Deported?" Maisy echoed. "What the hell does that mean? Deported *where*?"

The older man frowned at her. "Nowhere good, I can tell you that. And don't think I didn't notice you three aren't wearing your wrist units." He shook a finger at Maisy. "Best to just turn yourselves in."

"Turn ourselves in? We're not criminals!" Maisy protested. "And you just said they're sending people *nowhere good*." She glanced down to see the alarmed expression on Joanie's face and squeezed her hand. "It'll be okay," Maisy whispered.

The man shrugged indifferently and began unpacking a box onto a display, obviously done with the conversation and with them. Maisy stared at him in frustration for a moment before turning away.

As Maisy towed the kids toward the edge of the bodega, raised voices rang out again. From the direction they'd come, CSS officers were marching a line of people with red wrist units down the center of the corridor, each one wearing plastisteel cuffs. Ducking back into the shop, Maisy hustled the kids down an empty aisle and quietly slipped to the back of the store.

The manager had left the door to the storage room open. Maisy glanced back to see him moving toward the front of the store to investigate the ruckus. Holding firmly to Joanie and Leo, Maisy slipped through the door into the back room. Quickly they made their way to the utility corridor, Maisy remembered from her last visit. She struggled for a moment to figure out how many days ago that was, and then gave it up.

"Elevator," she said to the kids, gesturing to the right. They made their way to the door and Maisy tapped the panel, relieved when the door opened immediately. Stepping inside, the three of them turned to face the door and Maisy selected B deck on the controls. Nothing happened.

She hit the button for every upper level. Nothing.

"Crap."

Maisy shot a guilty look at Joanie, then tried the controls again, hitting floors at random. Unlike her last visit, nothing seemed to be working.

Her finger hovered over the button for H deck and she recalled the conversation outside of the Tow. Skipping down to the maintenance level, Maisy tapped the option for sub level one. This time the doors slid shut and the car moved down.

9

As above so below

The elevator doors opened to a crosshatch of metal bars and Maisy panicked. She grabbed at the bars and they moved easily. Maisy let out a relieved breath as they slid to the left, the gate folding in on itself. The metal was warm in her hand and a rush of heat flowed into the elevator.

Taking a deep breath to calm her nerves, she glanced down at her two charges. Reaching for Joanie's hand, Maisy said, "Hold onto Leo's hand and don't let go, okay?" Checking that her bag was still firmly secured to her back, she led the way out of the elevator and into the bowels of the Citadel.

After the stark white plasticore walls of all of the decks above, the gray metal corridor seemed dark and dirty. Beneath their feet was metal grating. There wasn't enough light to see what was below that but it didn't look solid. Pipes hung from the ceiling at irregular intervals and bundles of wire draped alongside them.

They came to a junction and Maisy considered each tunnel before continuing forward. If the sublevel mimicked the layout of the residential levels above, they should still be headed toward the central hub.

Heat seemed to radiate from the floor and walls and soon all three of them were dripping with sweat. Maisy's hair clung to her scalp and she knew her curls were getting tighter in response to the humidity in the air. She was suddenly envious of Joanie's braids and Leo's short cut.

Crushed under the weight of her responsibility for the kids, Maisy took slow, even breaths. In the back of her head, she kept rehashing her decisions. Should she have let the CSS take them into custody? Her instincts at the time had screamed *no*. But now her gut had led her into this seventh level of hell with two kids that really needed their moms. *So that made three of us*, Maisy thought.

Shaking off her doubts, Maisy ducked into an alcove and pulled the kids in behind her. Some kind of storage space, the doorless room was set back from the corridor and provided at least minimal protection if anyone passed by.

"Let's take a break, guys." Maisy took her bag from her shoulder. There were boxes stacked along the edge of the room and she pulled a couple over to make seating. Joanie and Leo collapsed gratefully onto them.

Maisy rummaged into her bag, pulling out a can of water and three bars.

"Dig in," she said, distributing the bars.

Joanie tore into her bar with a semblance of her usual gusto, but Leo just looked down at his in his hands, his face blank. He'd been on his own for a couple of days and Maisy could imagine how stressful that must have been. After a moment he removed the wrapper with slow, precise movements, and ate his bar, head down.

"What are we going to do, Maze?" asked Joanie.

"Technically," Maisy replied, "we're hiding." She smiled at Joanie, coaxing a tiny smile in return. "I didn't want to go with those CSS guys. And there aren't a lot of places to go on a station."

"We can't stay down here forever, though, right?" Joanie gestured with the empty bar wrapper in her hand. "We need more food. And water."

"I don't know what's down here," Maisy admitted. "We'll walk to the atrium—or what would be the atrium—and see what's there. Then we'll figure out our next step."

"Do you think those guys took my mom?" Leo asked, almost in a whisper. "And Joanie's mom?"

Maisy hesitated for a moment. "Yes," she said honestly. "I know Joanie's mom would have come back for her unless someone was stopping her and I bet the same is true for your mom too."

"So if we let those guys catch us, they might take us to where our moms are....right?" Leo said hopefully.

"They might," Maisy admitted.

Joanie and Leo exchanged a look, some silent communication passing between them.

"I think we should go back," Joanie said, Leo nodding in agreement.

Maisy sat back, shocked.

"I know those guys may be bad guys, but if we're going to be in trouble then I'd rather be in trouble with my mom," Joanie said firmly.

"I'm not one hundred percent sure that they have your mom—" Maisy started.

"But you think they do?" Joanie interrupted.

"Yes," Maisy confirmed reluctantly.

"And my mom?" added Leo quietly.

Maisy looked at his face, drawn and pale. She was much less sure about what might have happened to Leo's mom, but she couldn't say that. There was no point. So she just nodded.

"Then we want to go back," Joanie said, her voice quiet but full of resolve.

Maisy looked at Joanie, then Leo, mulling over their logic. *They weren't wrong.*

"Okay," she said finally. "Let's keep going toward the atrium and see if the elevator is there. If it isn't, we'll come back to the freight elevator. Deal?" Both kids nodded, pleased with the plan.

Maisy collected their wrappers and finished off the last drop of water from the can and put the trash back into her bag before swinging it back onto her shoulders. "Ready?" she asked. Both kids nodded solemnly and Maisy led the way back into the main corridor.

After a few minutes they came to a T intersection. Following her memory, Maisy turned left. This hallway was much wider and didn't feel quite as claustrophobic, although the low ceiling was still dripping with pipes and wires.

Up ahead, the right side of the corridor opened into a large control room of some sort. There were stations and large screens, all dark. There were cups and scattered personal items sitting on the surfaces, but no people.

Maisy walked over to one of the stations and tapped experimentally on the panel but there was no response. Everything appeared to be dead. Walking over to another desk, Maisy lifted up a sheet of old fashioned paper, covered in hand written notes. Judging by the daily output schedule and capacity numbers, this control room had housed the management of the ore processing plant. Obviously the plant was still running. Where was the team?

The only active panel in the room was a vertical screen showing a rainbow of status lights. Maisy walked closer and leaned in to read the labels by each indicator. Numbered generators, intake assemblies, processors. These were the guts of the station, all showing green, yellow, or red. There were an alarming number of red.

As Maisy stepped away from the panel she glimpsed a flash of movement from the corner of her eye. There was an alcove in the adjacent wall but when she whipped her head around to look, it seemed empty. Walking closer Maisy realized the recess extended behind the wall. Glancing back to see the children watching her, Maisy raised her hand for them to stay put, and walked silently into the hidden room.

The recess turned into a hallway to the right, leading to a darkened doorway. Maisy hesitated, thinking hard and wishing she had the light built into her wrist unit. If she approached the darkened doorway she'd be completely visible to whoever was inside but unable to see them.

Stopping just inside the alcove, facing the doorway, Maisy called out in her girliest voice. "Hello? Is anyone in there?" Maisy took a half step back. "We're lost. Can you help us?" Stepping back completely out of the alcove and into the main room, Maisy walked over the stand in front of the kids.

From around the hidden corner came the quiet shuffle of footsteps and a tousled red head appeared. It belonged to a girl who might be a couple of years older than Maisy but a couple of centimeters shorter, holding a little boy on her hip with peachfuzz on the top of his head the same shade of red.

"You're lost too?" Maisy commiserated. The girl with red hair nodded while the baby stared at Maisy solemnly.

Before Maisy could stop her, Joanie approached the girl and offered her finger to the little boy. He took it without hesitation, giving her a big toothless grin in return.

"We're not really lost," the redhead said, her face flushed from the heat. "I know exactly where we are. I just have no idea where to go from here."

Maisy nodded, "Yeah, we're in the same boat." She gestured at Joanie, who was busy cooing at the baby. "This is Joanie." Looking over her shoulder to find Leo hanging back, Maisy reached out a hand. He stepped forward gratefully and took it, allowing himself to be pulled into her side. "And this is Leo." Looking back at the other girl, she finished, "And I'm Maisy."

"Everyone calls her Maze," Joanie announced, not taking her eyes from the baby.

"Cute kid." Maisy smiled at Joanie who was making faces at the baby.

"It's not mine," the other girl replied. "Well, I guess technically it is. He is. This is Joey, my little brother. I'm Lori." The girl rolled her eyes at herself and gave a self-deprecating smile. Maisy returned the smile.

"How did you get down here?" Maisy asked quietly.

Lori tossed her head to move her hair behind her shoulders and out of the baby's grasp. "The CSS arrested my dad. Then they came knocking on our door and my mom told me to take the baby and hide."

"Where did you hide if they were already at the door?" Maisy asked, confused.

"My mom is the senior maintenance engineer. She popped one of the plasticore wall panels off and shoved us inside." The girl stopped and turned back toward the hidden room. "I don't think it's safe to be in the open. I can show you where we've been hiding."

Maisy nodded and they followed Lori back into the alcove. They stopped at the doorway to the darkened room and watched Lori disappear inside. A moment later, a lamp flared to life within, revealing a small office space. The desk had been set on its front side and pushed against one wall and there was a blanket and a toy bear in the space it created. Next to the makeshift crib was another blanket and a small pile of protein bars and water cans.

"Nice little nest you have here," Maisy drawled.

Lori shrugged. "I'm doing the best I can."

"You're doing better than I am," Maisy told her honestly, meeting her gaze.

Lori smiled sadly and folded gracefully to the floor, cradling the baby in her lap. Joanie followed, her finger still in little Joey's iron grip. Maisy lowered herself as smoothly as she could, pulling Leo down beside her. "How long have you been holed up here?"

"I'm not really sure. It was Tuesday morning—just before first shift—when the CSS came to our unit. What's today?" she asked.

Maisy thought for a moment. "I think it's Thursday...It's been a really long week."

"You're not kidding," Lori said, with a tight laugh. If there was a slight hysterical edge to the other girl's laughter, Maisy wasn't going to point it out.

"So, your parents knew what was coming?" Maisy prompted.

"Oh, yeah," Lori replied, wiping sweat from her face. "My mom is the local union rep on station. Or she was. Citatech completely disbanded the local unit and forbade union participation by Citadel employees."

"Wow. That sounds flat out illegal."

"It is!" Lori agreed. "My mom went supernova. She was ready to start fabricating pitchforks and torches. My dad talked her down but I know they had a meeting with the station chief that did not go well."

Lori's eyes had a far away look. "My mom tried to submit a formal complaint and realized we were locked out of the comms system. She put a message on a thumbdrive and sent my dad to give it to the captain of a transport heading back to Earth. One of the guys in her crew told her that the CSS was arresting people and they picked up my dad."

Lori was lost in the telling of her story, fear in her eyes.

"Then the CSS came. I could hear them yelling. It didn't even make sense for them to arrest my dad. He's not even a member of the union." Lori shook her head in confusion. "I'm not even sure what my mom was saying. Something about Citatech getting rid of people."

Lori looked at Maisy, her eyes beseeching. "But I'm sure that doesn't mean what it sounds like, right? How could it?"

Maisy looked down at Joey, now gnawing on Joanie's finger. Joanie seemed to be completely absorbed in stroking the ginger babyfluff on his head. Maisy looked at Leo, sitting on her right. His eyes were wide and it was obvious he was listening to their conversation and reaching his own conclusions. Maisy put an arm around his shoulder and pulled him closer. He angled his head into her chest and quietly shook.

Crap, Maisy thought.

"I'm sure they're okay." Maisy looked at Lori and squeezed Leo's small shoulder. "All of them are okay."

"There's only one way to find out," piped up a little voice. Joanie was looking at her calmly, her finger still held captive by little Joey.

"We have to go back up," Joanie said in what Maisy was coming to think of as her "firm voice".

"Your parents were arrested too?" Lori asked.

"My mom went to buy us tickets to Earth and didn't come back," explained Joanie. "And it would definitely take a lot of men with shocksticks to keep my mom from coming back for me."

"Damn straight," Maisy agreed, causing Joanie to burst into giggles. Even Leo looked up with a small smile on his face.

"My mom wouldn't leave me either," Leo said quietly. He didn't have the forceful confidence of Joanie, but his faith in his mom was strong enough that he was terrified of what had happened to keep her from him.

"We'll find her, Leo," Maisy said. "We'll find all of them."

"We aren't going to find them down here, Maze," Joanie pointed out.

"You're right, kid." Maisy sighed. "We're going back up," she said to Lori. "Do you want to come with us?"

Lori looked down at her little brother nestled in her lap and wiped sweat from his little face. Looking back up, Lori smiled sadly. "We can't stay down here forever and Joanie is right. We need to know what happened."

"And we should all be together," Joanie said earnestly. "If bad things are going to happen then it's better if we're all together."

Lori nodded, at peace with her decision. "What's your plan?" she asked, looking at Maisy.

"We were going to go to the center of this level and see if there is an access there. If not, we're going to go back to the freight elevators. That's how we got here."

"The center of this level is the main control room for the station mechanics. But it's been mothballed, just like the ore processing control room out there."

"How did you guys get down here?" Maisy asked.

"We took the service stairs that connect all of the levels. There are four sets, one near each elevator. There are two maintenance elevators and another freight elevator," Lori explained. Maisy was impressed with her knowledge of the station.

"Maze," Leo pulled on Maisy's sleeve. "Can we have another water? I'm so hot."

"Of course." Maisy pulled another can from her bag. She popped the top and handed it to Leo, who took a long drink and passed the can to Joanie. Looking at him closely in the light of the little lamp, Maisy was alarmed to note how flushed he had become. His pale cheeks were splotched with red and his blond hair was stuck to his forehead. Holding a hand to her own forehead, Maisy realized the heat had increased noticeably while they were talking.

"I think it's time to go, guys."

In silent agreement, they all rose to their feet. Turning to reach behind the laid over desk, Lori came up with a bag of her own and stuffed Joey's little bear into it.

"I can carry Joey," Joanie offered hopefully.

Lori smiled down at the little girl but shook her head. "He's a lot heavier than he looks."

"Maybe you could carry Joey's bag," Maisy suggested, sharing a smile with Lori.

Weight redistributed, they set off back toward the freight elevator with a tentative plan in place. If they couldn't use the elevator, they'd use the stairs located nearby. They walked in silence, foreheads glistening with sweat.

As they rounded a bend in the corridor, a man and a woman wearing black coveralls plowed headfirst into the group, the man tumbling to the floor as Maisy rebounded off the wall. As Maisy caught herself and regained her equilibrium, the man scrambled up, panting. The woman clutched at his arm as everyone looked at each other for a moment, assessing their situations.

"CSS is right behind us," the woman said, urging the man forward. "You kids need to run." Warning given, the two stumbled back into a run and disappeared around the corner. Maisy and Lori exchanged worried looks.

Maisy acknowledged Joanie's point that it was better if they were with her mom, and this sub level was rapidly becoming uninhabitable...but her instincts wouldn't allow her to stand here while the CSS descended upon them.

Lori must have reached the same conclusion because she hefted Joey higher in her arms and began running back the way they'd come, after the man and woman.

"Come on, guys." Maisy pushed Joanie and Leo ahead of her. They quickly passed the ore processing control center and Maisy thought for a moment of trying to hide in the dark alcove, but she knew that was no longer a viable option. They needed a plan and she didn't have one.

As they entered the wider corridor near the center of the level, two people appeared from another hallway and began running alongside them. Glancing over Maisy was surprised that they were young, maybe her age.

"Are you running from CSS?" Maisy asked, breathing hard.

The boy next to her startled hard, almost tripping. He regained his rhythm and looked at her as if he'd just noticed there were other people running too. "Yeah! They're right behind us!" he panted.

They'd almost caught up with the couple who had run into them earlier. The man was obviously limping and the woman had a shoulder under his arm. Another man burst from a hallway on the right, almost sending the couple to the floor again, but they kept their feet this time.

"They're herding us." Maisy looked to Lori, trying to control her breathing. The girl nodded, adjusting her grip on her brother. A wave of calm washed over Maisy as she accepted the inevitable. She touched Joanie and Leo's shoulders and slowed to a fast walk, letting the other people in the hallway pull ahead. Soon there were more. A couple of them were limping or looked like they'd been in a fight. Everyone looked severely overheated, tired and dirty. Beside her, Lori had also slowed, Joey resting his head on her shoulder.

"It's going to be okay, guys," Maisy said. "Just stay calm and follow directions. We're going to stay together, and if things get crazy we'll just sit down out of the way and wait for everything to calm down." The kids looked more tired than afraid at this point, and Maisy could relate.

As their party of five approached the central hub of the station—what would be the atrium area in the residential levels—Maisy was shocked at how many people had made it down to this level. They were milling around what appeared to be another abandoned control center, voices raised in panic as they tried to figure out an escape route.

Maisy and Lori moved behind a large console as the CSS officers emerged from each of the main corridors in what must have been an orchestrated maneuver. In full armor with featureless opaque black helmets, shocksticks in hand, the CSS were terrifying figures. Joanie and Leo clung to Maisy, trembling.

A man standing near the entrance to one of the tunnels lunged forward, knocking the nearest CSS officer off his feet. Immediately three other officers had their sticks raised and took the man to the floor. In seconds he was lying unconscious, face down on the deck, each wrist encircled in a thick band of unbreakable plastisteel alloy.

There were a few other scuffles around the room but the heat and exertion had worn everyone down. Most people lined up docilely and allowed themselves to be cuffed. There were several teenagers in the crowd and a young boy. Maisy watched carefully to see how they were treated by the CSS. The kid wasn't cuffed, but the teenagers were. There were no other babies besides Joey. All of the other teenagers were boys.

"Stay close," Maisy whispered to Lori, who nodded. She suspected if they presented as a unit they might get away without cuffs. If they did cuff anyone, it would be Maisy. Not ideal, but not the end of the world.

The five of them huddled quietly at the side of the room, Joey fast asleep on Lori's shoulder as the CSS officers lined up their prisoners and began marching them down one of the corridors in groups. There were only a handful of refugees left when two CSS officers finally made their way over to them. Their small group straightened and calmly waited for the officers to speak.

"Come this way," one of the helmeted men instructed.

Now that they were hot and tired and no longer being chased, the walk down the corridor from the central hub of the station to the freight elevators took quite a bit longer. Lori shifted Joey's weight from side to side and the kids dragged their feet in exhaustion.

They reached the freight elevator to find another group already waiting. The elevator arrived, the handcuffed people were piled in unceremoniously, and it departed again. Maisy and Lori exchanged worried looks as they waited for its return. A couple of minutes later, the doors opened with a *ding*. One of the officers pulled back the metal gate and waved their group into the box. They crowded to the rear of the car, pressing their backs against the wall and watched as the officer pulled the gate closed and selected the first residential level. His wrist unit flashed green and the car began moving.

The car stopped again almost immediately, opening to more officers standing at attention, waiting for them.

"Last group," one of the officers announced.

Maisy led the children out of the elevator and followed the officers through the atrium to a residential corridor. The shops on both sides were closed and looked they would never open again. All of the security gates were shut tight and the windows dark. The signs and kiosks were gone and everything seemed abandoned.

A couple more turns and they were brought to a nondescript door. The officer tapped the panel and it slid open to reveal an empty unit, a little bit bigger than Maisy or Sue's but without the loft space above.

"In there," the officer commanded and they piled into the small space.

Turning back toward the door and the officers who were still standing outside of the entrance, Maisy asked in a quiet and calm voice, "Can you help us find our parents?"

"Just wait here," a voice responded from the opaque helmet.

"Are you sending us somewhere? Can you tell us where?" Maisy asked, working hard to keep her voice calm and even.

"No." The officer stepped back and the door slid shut.

10

Bon voyage

After a sleepless night, Maisy found herself sitting at a small table in their makeshift cell. They'd all been too tired to do much exploring the night before, but this morning Maisy had cataloged the food in the unit and put together a somewhat healthy breakfast for everyone.

Lori had dark bruises under her eyes and Maisy could tell the stress of the last few days was taking its toll. Leo was looking much better this morning. Joanie's braids were a bit worse for wear, but otherwise the kids had bounced back amazingly well. Joey had proved to be the most resilient of them all and was happily cooing to himself as he ate his reconstituted veggie mush.

Maisy and Lori stood at the kitchen counter, looking at the alarmingly small pile of food they had available. Between what each of them had brought in their bags and the box of cereal they'd found in the back of one of the cabinets, they wouldn't last long. *At least it isn't as hot here.*

"Where was the panel that your mother removed in your unit?" Maisy asked Lori.

"We had a two bedroom unit and it was between the bathroom and the bedrooms. But it didn't go anywhere. I just hid in there until the CSS left and then I came out." Lori shrugged apologetically.

"It's okay." They had decided to cooperate, and for now that meant staying in this room. Maisy really wanted to have options. Walking over to the door, she tapped the panel as she had the night before, expecting nothing. Maisy was turning away when the door slid open.

Whipping her head around, she came face to face with the reflective black visage of a CSS helmet.

A hand shot out, thrusting a thin silicone bag at her. Maisy grabbed it reflexively and the door slid shut again. *What the...?*

She turned back to the room to see everyone staring at her, mouths open. She moved quickly to the table and placed the bag on the top, reaching inside to remove a handful of baby food containers and at least a dozen protein bars.

"Well," Maisy said in surprise, "I guess we won't starve!" She barked out a laugh involuntarily, still reeling from the abrupt appearance of the food.

"That was weird, right?" Lori asked.

"Yes. Yes, it was," Maisy confirmed. "But then again, every-thing seems to be, these days."

Joanie pulled at Maisy's sleeve. "Can I have another bar, Maze?"

"Yup," she replied.

"Leo," Maisy asked, "would you like another bar too?" Leo nodded quietly and she passed out bars to the kids and one to Lori, who accepted it gratefully. Maisy grabbed one for herself and they all sat in companionable silence, eating their processed meal bars while Joey cleaned up the last of his veggies.

When they were finished, Maisy and Lori put all of the food into one bag and placed it near the door. Joanie led an effort to dismantle the benches in the small unit to make an enclosure for Joey. Leo seemed content to follow her directions and be-fore long they had everything set up to Joanie's specifications.

Leaning back against the wall, Maisy patted the space next to her and Leo sat down with a sigh. It was only mid-day but they were all exhausted.

"Hey, Leo." Maisy remembered the question she wanted to ask, "What's your mom's name?"

Leo looked confused. Maisy fully expected him to answer, "mom," but after a moment, the gears shifted and he said, "Jane".

Maisy nodded encouragingly. "Can you tell me what she looks like?"

"She looks like me," Leo replied solemnly. "Our hair and our eyes and our skin are all exactly the same." Leo's lower lip trembled and Maisy wrapped an arm around his shoulder and pulled him in for a hug.

"What about your parents?" Maisy asked Lori, sitting across from her.

"My dad has red hair," Lori said, waving vaguely toward her own head. "My mom has gray hair, really short. What about your parents?"

"I don't think they're here." Maisy's gaze moved around the room. "But your parents should be, and Joanie's mom. So we need to keep an eye out."

"My mom looks like me too," Joanie said. "But she has short hair. But it's just like mine and she's really, really pretty."

"We'll find her," Maisy told the little girl. "Joanie's mom's name is Sue. What are your parents' names?" she asked Lori.

"Carl and Sonia."

"Okay," Maisy said. "We'll find them."

Joey chose that moment to laugh and clap, startling everyone out of their serious expressions. Maisy tried to smile at the little boy, exhaustion wearing her down.

"Let's try to get some sleep." A chorus of murmured agreements met Maisy's suggestion and before long they were all lying quietly in the middle of the living room, lights at twenty percent.

Within minutes, all three kids were out for the count.

"Maze," Lori said quietly, "What did you mean that your parents aren't here? They're not on the Citadel?"

Maisy pressed her lips together for a moment. "My mom died on Earth. I was here with my dad, but something happened."

"Something on the station?"

"No, out on the rim somewhere." Maisy stared up at the ceiling. "My dad is a marine and I don't think he came back from his last mission. But comms are out, so I'm not sure." She turned to look over at Lori above the heads of the sleeping kids.

"But I just have a feeling, you know?" There was understanding in Lori's eyes and Maisy looked up at the ceiling again, trying not to think.

Maisy's eyes opened and she took stock of her surroundings. The lights in the unit were still low and everyone else appeared to be asleep. Listening hard, Maisy tried to figure out what had pulled her from her sleep.

After a moment, the sound came again. The units weren't soundproof and footsteps were moving down the hall. More footsteps passed them a couple of minutes later, one set firm and synchronized, the other shuffling and disjointed.

Jumping to her feet, Maisy crossed the small room to crouch beside Lori and touch her shoulder. "Wake up. I think this is it."

Lori stared blankly at Maisy for a moment, then jumped up. She grabbed Joey and a clean diaper while Maisy shook Joanie and Leo awake and ushered them into the bathroom one at a time. Then Maisy held Joey while Lori took her turn. Lori slipped out and Maisy slipped in and peed in record time. The noises in the hallway were getting louder. It sounded like they were emptying the rooms one by one. Footsteps up the hall, a larger group down the hall, the cycle repeating.

Standing by the door, bag over her shoulder, the others lined up behind her, Maisy listened and tried to pinpoint which room was next. "I think that was next door," Maisy said quietly over her shoulder. The kids vibrated with tension but they all seemed to be in better shape after a day of rest. Whatever was next, they were as ready as they'd ever be.

The door to the unit slid open and two CSS officers stood in the hallway, gesturing them forward. One walked ahead of Maisy and she followed him down the hall. She glanced back quickly to see Joanie and Leo behind her, followed by Lori holding Joey. The second officer walked behind Lori, his shockstick in his hands. Maisy met Lori's eyes briefly, and turned back around.

Past the officer in front of her, other groups were moving down the hallway. Everyone was being very quiet. There were several people with obvious injuries. One woman cradled what looked like a broken arm, her face pale. A few were still wearing cuffs. Maisy searched their faces for Sue or anyone who might match the other parents' descriptions.

As they reached the end of the hall and turned to the right, Maisy realized they were heading toward the loading bays. She'd traveled to this part of the station to visit her dad's ship once and it seemed familiar. The station had only one dock, used by passenger transports, freighters, and the marine corvettes. The passenger transports had their own flyways that connected to the upper decks of the station and funneled people directly to the residential areas.

The CSS officers were leading their prisoners to the cargo entrance of the dock where the non-passenger traffic was moored. Her eyes searched for the *Sky* but she knew it wouldn't be there. Another corvette was at the far end of the bay, and a large cargo shuttle from a freighter. The ramp was down on the shuttle and people were being marched up it and into the belly of the large, boxy ship.

A man in wrist cuffs, already sporting a black eye, flung himself away from the group and was immediately snagged by an officer and bounced down onto the deck. The featureless black helmet gave no sign of emotion as the officer bound the man's ankles with a plastisteel zipcord. Another CSS stepped up and the two of them carried the man up the ramp like a sack of potatoes.

Joanie's hand reached for Maisy's and she gripped it firmly. So far there'd been no sign of any of their parents and she knew the kids were losing hope. They also hadn't seen the other kids who had been picked up by the CSS the day before, so she knew there must be other prisoners, possibly already on the shuttle.

Some of the prisoners looked around desperately with wild eyes but no one else made a run for it. There was nowhere to go. They really were being deported.

Finally, their group walked up the ramp and into the cargo shuttle. Inside, it appeared to be a large featureless room, full of people in t-shirts and coveralls or utility pants, standing in small groups. Along one wall there were loaders docked into the wall. There were CSS agents arrayed along the far wall, weapons in hand. The left wall held a staircase and Maisy realized it led to the ship's cockpit, which hung over the bay door.

"Last group," said a voice behind them, and Maisy turned. She assumed the voice came from the helmeted officer behind Lori, since no one else was there. The black uniformed figure slammed a fist on the door panel and the ramp rose, sealing them all in together. When Maisy turned back, the officer she'd been following had joined the line at the front of the room.

A moment later, the deck beneath her feet began to vibrate and there were murmurs of alarm from the prisoners.

"Where are you taking us?" It was the man with the black eye, who was now sitting on the deck, still bound hand and feet. "Are we going back to Earth?"

No one answered him.

Moving slowly, Maisy led her group slowly to the alcove under the stairs, keeping to the edge of the crowd and watching the CSS officers to see if they would object. The blank black surfaces of their helmets gave nothing away, but no one made a movement.

When they reached the stairs, Maisy sat down in the space beneath them, pulling Joanie down with her. She motioned Leo and Lori to sit as well and they all huddled in the small semi-protected space as the rumble beneath the deck increased to a roar and the ship began to move.

There were cries from the crowd and people clutched at each other for stability as the ship left the floor of the dock. Finally, people seemed to realize the danger and began dropping to the deck. In seconds, the only ones still standing were the CSS officers. Without windows, Maisy had no way of knowing exactly where they were, but she imagined they were near to exiting the station. A moment later, the sound of the engines seemed to even out and Maisy took that to mean that they had entered space.

In theory, shuttles belonged to ships. Were they being taken to a freighter? One thing was for sure, this was not a long distance vehicle. They weren't going back to Earth in this shuttle.

Still holding Joanie's hand, Maisy scanned the faces in the bay. Now that everyone was sitting, it was a little easier to scan the crowd. There was no sign of Sue, no flares of red hair except for Lori, sitting next to her. But near the far edge of the space, there was a flash of very pale hair. Maisy craned her neck to get a better view, but couldn't make out any other features. She was tempted to try to call out, but the silent CSS officers gave her pause.

Sitting back against the wall, she looked down at Joanie, snug against her side. Leo was tucked in between Joanie and Lori and Joey was asleep and drooling in Lori's lap.

Without her wrist unit it was hard to keep track of the time going by, but Maisy was cold and stiff when the sound of the engines changed. She and Lori shared a look. Joey was still sleeping and Leo and Joanie had both dozed off. She knew it would be a while still until they docked with whatever vessel they were meeting, so by unspoken agreement the two older girls let the younger children sleep.

The other passengers were stirring and low conversations circulated through the open space. Listening quietly and watching expressions, Maisy reached the conclusion that everyone was just as clueless as she was.

Another twenty minutes or so passed before the sound of the engines changed again, and the vibration of the floors became stronger. Maisy imagined the intersystem drive had likely been cut and they were operating by thrusters now as they approached their rendezvous. Suddenly, the engine sounds totally cut off.

Magnetics, thought Maisy. *We're in.*

In *what* was the question.

As the tractor pulled their shuttle into position, there was no vibration. Their engines were off and the mags were smooth. Within minutes, the entire shuttle shook as they were set down on a solid surface. Joanie and Leo were jostled by the landing enough to begin moving and Maisy helped them to their feet as Lori rose as well, hefting the still sleeping Joey.

Once she was on her feet, Maisy searched the shuffling crowd for the blonde head she'd seen earlier. With most of the passengers still seated, she had a much better vantage point and spotted the figure almost immediately. It was a woman and she did look the right age. She was still sitting on the deck, her head cradled in her hands, her shoulders rounded.

"Leo." Maisy gave a small nod toward the crowd. "Do you see that lady over there?"

Leo caught the implication immediately and his eyes lit up. Maisy groaned internally, hoping she wasn't raising his hopes for nothing. Meanwhile, Leo had abandoned any attempt at subtlety and was craning his neck desperately to see the woman Maisy had indicated.

"Mom?" Then a moment later, much louder, "Mom!"

Across the open bay, the woman's head whipped up, her red rimmed eyes flashing in their direction. Scrambling to her feet, she pushed and stumbled her way through the crowd toward them. Maisy held Leo in place and watched the CSS officers against the back wall of the shuttle, but they didn't seem inclined to interfere.

11

Shit, meet fan

As Leo's mom cleared the edge of the crowd Maisy released her hold on the boy's shoulder and he flew into his mother's arms, both of them sobbing. Maisy swallowed hard, holding her eyes wide. She took deep breaths and cleared her mind of everything but her happiness for Leo and his mom.

Hearing a sniff beside her, Maisy looked over to see Lori quietly crying into Joey's hair. The little boy was awake and confused and looked ready to start bawling, his little chin wobbling.

Crap, Maisy thought. She hated to interrupt their reunion, but the doors would open at any moment and they all needed to be ready for whatever faced them next.

"Jane?" Leo's mom looked up, her eyes glistening. "I'm Maisy. Leo has been staying with us. He said you guys got separated?" Maisy prompted.

Jane pulled herself together visibly, wiping her eyes and running a hand through her short hair. She anchored one arm around Leo's shoulders, his face still buried against her. Maisy motioned her into their little alcove under the stairs and Jane joined them gratefully.

"I'm Joanie," the little girl introduced herself. "I'm Leo's friend." Joanie put her hand on Leo's back and he raised his head enough to give her a wet smile. It looked very, very similar to the one on his mom's face and Maisy's heart gave another lurch in her chest.

"We ran into each other outside the bodega on G deck," Maisy said.

Jane smiled down at Leo. "That was such a good idea!" she told him. "I would have looked for you there." Her smile faded and Maisy could see again how pale she was. "I was arrested by the CSS and I had no way to reach you, baby. I was so worried..." Jane looked on the verge of tears again, so Maisy quickly jumped in.

"We've been together, taking care of each other. This is Lori," Maisy introduced. The other girl had dried her eyes and was making an effort to pull herself together.

"We had cereal!" Joanie announced, and everyone smiled.

Above their heads, feet hit the staircase as the shuttle's crew left the bridge. To their right, the shuttle door opened from the top with a grinding noise, giving everyone their first glimpse of their surroundings. Maisy and her small group huddled in the relative safety of their little alcove under the stairs as the murmur of voices reached a crescendo.

The open door revealed a row of black helmets standing before the shuttle. As the ramp thudded to the deck, the passengers glanced nervously between the CSS officers behind them, at the back of the shuttle, and those before them, at the foot of the ramp.

As one, the CSS at the back of the shuttle drew their shock-sticks and walked forward toward the passengers. Crying out in fear, the men and women had no choice but to move down the ramp. As the first prisoners approached the end of the ramp, the officers there finally moved aside, forming a funnel to move the people away from the shuttle.

Maisy and her group were herded down the ramp and into what turned out to be a huge cargo bay, nearly as big as the one on the station. The cargo shuttle was docked next to a nearly identical ship and there were pallets anchored to the deck throughout the bay, many of them stacked halfway to the ceiling. Maisy rounded a huge array of boxes piled twice as tall as she was. There was a group ahead of them and she realized immediately that this must be the rest of the missing station residents.

Maisy gripped Joanie's hand as she scanned the crowd, her eyes flitting over each person as she looked for Sue—or any familiar face. Beside her Lori was desperately doing the same.

Lori gasped and took off running into the crowd. Joanie pulled Maisy after her. "We have to stay together, Maze!" Joanie yelled over her shoulder and Maisy followed in her wake.

Looking back over her shoulder, Maisy motioned to Leo's mom, Jane. "Come with us," Maisy said urgently. Jane hesitated but Leo followed Maisy, pulling his mom behind him. Turning forward again, Maisy had lost track of Lori but Joanie moved with purpose so Maisy trusted that the little girl knew where she was going.

When they breached the edge of the crowd Maisy finally caught sight of Lori as the red-haired girl flung herself to her knees beside a woman lying on the deck. In her arms, Joey was crying and struggling, thrusting himself at the woman, who didn't move.

A wiry man with thinning red hair in a halo around his head was kneeling on the other side of the woman. He reached across her unconscious body to grip Joey and Lori in an awkward but fierce embrace.

Joanie fell down on her knees next to Lori, looking down at the unconscious woman. Joanie touched Lori's arm gently. "Is your mom okay?" Joanie asked quietly and Maisy's heart clenched like a fist in her chest.

Lori pulled back from her father's embrace and looked down at her mother, Joey still cradled in her arms. "Mom?" Her dad reached across and lifted Joey from her arms, clasping the baby to his chest, his face buried in the peach fuzz hair a shade lighter than his own.

Joanie and Maisy sat frozen as Lori touched her mom's shoulder, then her cheek. Finally, the woman's eyes fluttered and drifted open slowly. It took her a moment to focus on Lori's face, but when she did, recognition washed over her expression and she was suddenly more alert. Her hand lifted slowly and Lori gripped it.

"Oh, baby," Lori's mother moaned softly. "I'm so sorry."

"For what?" Lori asked, confused.

"For leaving you. All of you." Her eyes drifted shut again and it seemed to take her a huge effort to open them the second time. Lori looked up at her dad for an explanation and did a double take. He was covered in bruises and his shirt was torn and burned in places. Lori looked down at her mother, who was in the same condition, an oozing red welt across her forehead.

"What happened?" Lori said in shock. Her dad lifted his head and Lori recoiled at his expression. He looked beaten, in every sense of the word. Tears were running down his face from his sunken eyes.

"It was the CSS," her father said baldly. "They've converted all of the contracts on the station into nothing more than indentured servitude. When they took us into custody they tried to get your mom to give union approval. People were objecting and they wanted her to rubber stamp the mods since she was the senior rep on station."

Lori's dad looked down at his wife, who was unconscious again, his expression a mix of pride and pain.

"She refused." He looked back up at his daughter. "Instead, she organized the detainees into a revolt." Lori's dad smiled through his tears and Lori barked out a surprised laugh.

"Of course she did." Lori said, laying her hand carefully on the side of her mother's forehead that wasn't injured.

As quickly as it came, her father's smile slid from his face.

"I think she has internal bleeding," he said quietly. "They won't provide a medic and I don't know what to do, Lori."

Tears coated his cheeks and his voice was thick. "I'm so sorry, baby." He buried his face in the baby's hair again. Joey had calmed down and was nestled quietly against his father's chest.

Lori looked down at her mother again and gripped her hand firmly. "Mom?" she said. "Mom? Wake up, Mom." There was no response. A sob broke from Lori's throat and she hunched in on herself.

Joanie looked up at Maisy as tears fell silently from her wide eyes.

This is too much, Maisy thought.

She pulled the little girl into her side and held her while her little body was wracked in quiet sobs and laid her other hand on Lori's back, reluctant to intrude on her grief but wanting the other girl to know she was here. Suddenly, Leo was there too, wrapping his arms around Joanie and Maisy, one hand laid on Lori's back to mirror Maisy's.

"She's gone, baby," Lori's dad said quietly.

Joey began to cry, not understanding the emotions moving around him. The baby reached for Lori and she took him into her arms, sobbing. Lori turned toward Maisy and the children and they pulled her into their embrace. Maisy's eyes burned and she looked up at the ceiling of the cargo bay high above them, blinking hard and swallowing.

Jane, Leo's mom, caught Maisy's gaze. She was crouched behind her son, her hand on his back, while he clutched Joanie, both children crying.

"It's okay to cry," Jane said quietly, her face so similar to her son's.

"Not yet," Maisy said without thinking. "We're not out of the woods yet," she clarified. Jane nodded sadly, in agreement.

The people near their small group began moving and Maisy swallowed again and looked around, trying to figure out the disturbance. As the crowd flowed toward the bay doors, shouts came from the back of the room.

The zaps of shocksticks connecting with bodies jolted Maisy into action. She rose to her feet, pulling Joanie and Leo with her. When the three of them were up, she reached down and grabbed Lori's hand.

"We have to go."

Lori looked up at Maisy, her eyes blank.

"Come on, Lori. We can't stay here." Maisy pulled her to a standing position, holding onto her arm when she would have turned back to her mom.

"Lori." Her face softened. "I'm so sorry about your mom, but we need to go."

Lori nodded, still clutching Joey to her chest. She turned to her father, who was still kneeling. "Dad, we have to go."

The crowd was moving more quickly past them and the sounds of fighting were growing closer. The cargo bay was getting noisy when Maisy thought she heard her name.

"Maze! Maisy!" She whipped her head around, searching for the source of her name being called. A brown head bobbed through the crowd, getting closer.

Starting in recognition, Maisy cried out, "Sue!"

Joanie whipped around and tried to dart into the crowd, but Maisy held fast to the little girl's arm, not letting her go.

"She sees us," Maisy told her. "She's coming."

The smaller woman wove her way through the fast moving crowd. She disappeared and popped back up, much closer.

"Maisy!" Sue called, "Where is Joanie?" Her voice was desperate and came out in a sob.

"I've got her! She's here!" Maisy cried.

"Mom! Mom!" Joanie cried, trying desperately to wrest her arm from Maisy's grasp.

"Joanie, wait. She's coming." Maisy tracked Sue's movements, aware that they needed to be moving but afraid to leave the spot until Sue made it through the crowd. Finally, Sue burst through the stream of people and careened into Maisy.

"Maze!" she cried a split second before her eyes tracked down and took in the slight figure in Maisy's arms. "Joanie! Oh, thank god!" Sue scooped Joanie up and hugged her hard as the little girl wrapped her arms around her mother and hugged her back just as fiercely.

"We have to go!" Maisy cried. Her tears had finally broken free and were running down her face, but sounds of conflict were upon them. Maisy knew they had no choice but to try to outrun it.

A hand tugged Maisy's and she turned to find Leo pulling her in the direction of the crowd, his other hand held firmly by his mother. Maisy allowed herself to be moved a step toward the cargo bay exit, her head turned over her shoulder, checking to make sure the others were following.

Joanie had struggled down from her mother's embrace and with her feet back on the floor she was firmly pulling her mother after Maisy, but Lori had dropped back down to the floor, holding her father's hand where it rested on her mother's still chest.

"Lori!" Maisy cried. The older girl looked helplessly at Maisy, meeting her eyes over Joey's head. "Lori, we have to go!" Maisy pulled her hand from Leo's and dropped down to Lori's side. She scooped the baby from her arms and grabbed Lori's other hand, pulling her to her feet.

"Go, Lori," her father said as he struggled to his feet. "Go with them. Take care of Joey."

He met Maisy's gaze for a moment and then turned and hurled himself at one of the CSS officers now visible in the crowd.

"Dad!" Lori screamed, "No!" The officer flung off the smaller man and lifted his shockstick above his head. As his arm came down, the crowd surged, cutting them off from view.

Maisy hitched Joey onto her hip and pulled Lori away. She sobbed, turning to Maisy and Joey and stumbled, but kept her feet under her. Joanie was next to them, holding firmly onto her mom, and they rushed after Leo, whose mother was leading their retreat.

Realizing that Lori was running on her own, Maisy released her hand to shift Joey's weight to her other side. Up ahead a large doorway was creating a bottleneck in the crowd. They were running along the left edge of the crowd and would get stuck at the side of the doorway.

"Jane! Aim for the center of the door," Maisy called ahead. Jane didn't look back but she changed course, pulling Leo toward the center of the doorway. Maisy looked over at Joanie, running by her side. "Stay close, kid." Joanie nodded, looking determined and worried but calm.

All around them, men and women were running, panicked by the sounds of violence. As their group approached the doorway, the sides of the crowd squeezed in, forcing them apart. Maisy grabbed Leo's hand and held on. Looking at Lori over her shoulder, Maisy cried, "Grab my shirt and hold Joanie's hand!" Lori knotted her fist in the back of Maisy's shirt and reached for the little girl's hand. Joanie met Lori halfway, her other hand firmly in her mother's grip.

As the crowd squeezed in on either side, they narrowed to a string, holding on tight and Maisy held her breath as they made it through the doorway single file and into a large hallway. There were CSS Officers here as well, standing at stations along each wall.

A loud bang behind them caused the crowd to surge forward. There were cries of dismay behind them and Maisy fought the instinct to look back.

At a crossroads in the corridor the CSS were herding people to the right. The crowd was still moving quickly but the panic had subsided. Their group was able to relax, although Lori maintained her grip on Maisy's shirt.

Rounding another corner, the corridor ended in a large doorway. Filing through, the passengers looked around. They were obviously in some kind of cafeteria, already partially full of people. Jane made a beeline for the farthest end of the room and led them to an empty table.

Maisy sank gratefully into the bench, resting Joey on her lap and stretching out her abused arm and shoulder. Lori sat beside her, reaching for her brother. He threw his arms around her neck and the two huddled against each other. Sue and Joanie sat on Jane's other side, next to Leo.

The seven of them sat there silently as their breathing slowed. Around them, people were gathering at the tables, murmuring and speaking quietly with each other.

The last stragglers were finding their seats when a tall man in a black CSS uniform entered the cafeteria. His head was bare and his uniform was more ornate than that of the other officers. He wasn't wearing a helmet, although his bald head gleamed like one.

Walking to the front of the crowd, the man crossed his arms and scanned the distressed and exhausted faces dispassionately. Helmeted officers entered behind him and stood in a row, hands resting on their holstered shocksticks.

"I am Captain Tindell Burt, head of Citadel Security Services." His deep baritone cut through the room like a knife. "You have been removed from the Citadel and are no longer welcome in our facility," he announced. "At this time, the only transport available is this one. Welcome to the *Oro Zapato II*. This is a colony ship heading to a newly surveyed world in Sector 12. Congratulations, you are now colonists."

There were gasps among the crowd.

Beside Maisy, Sue jumped to her feet. "I have funds to purchase transport to Earth for myself and my child. We are not colonists!" Other voices called out similar statements and Sue stayed standing as the voices rose around her.

"We have money! We'll pay to go home!" was repeated by people throughout the cafeteria.

At the front of the room, the captain's expression didn't change. He stood there ignoring the shouts until they died down, then continued.

"You have all been tried and convicted of violations of the Citadel's penal code. As such, all of your accounts have been seized, your contracts have been terminated, and your residency permits have been revoked."

Voices cried out in horror and sobs echoed through the high-ceilinged room. The captain never faltered or acknowledged the people in the room in any way. Having delivered his announcement, he turned his back on the crowd and addressed the CSS officers arrayed behind him.

"Unit 7, you have been assigned to accompany these colonists to EV-12-761." There were no facial features visible through the shiny black helmets, but the officers stiffened. "Drop the *colonists* on the surface and return to the station."

The captain walked out of the room and past his officers who seemed frozen. There were more helmeted CSS officers in the hallway and they followed the captain as he disappeared from sight. Silence rang through the cafeteria for a moment and then everyone burst into sound at once. Some cried, some yelled. Maisy watched the members of Unit 7.

There were five members of the unit in the room and Maisy assumed there were more throughout the ship. They all appeared to be male, but it was hard to tell with the helmets. By their reaction, the news of their new assignment had come as a complete surprise. The officers were turning their heads minutely, looking at each other.

Maisy wanted to laugh at their predicament but she feared the onset of hysteria. For the moment, Unit 7's problems were their own and she needed to focus on the immediate future.

A faint vibration moved through the deck and Maisy wondered if the engines had been engaged. As abruptly as it began, the vibration stopped.

"Shuttle lifting off," Jane explained. Maisy gave a small nod of acknowledgement.

Sue was still standing and she looked down at Joanie, who sat between her and Maisy. "Stay with Maze, Joanie," she said as she walked forward. Joanie lurched up to follow her but Maisy pulled her back with an arm around her shoulder.

"Listen to your mom, kid," Maisy told her. "We need more information...." Maisy trailed off, wondering how Sue would approach the officers, whom it seemed had been abandoned along with them.

Sue had obviously been wearing her black coveralls and gray t-shirt for several days, since the last time they'd been together, but they were intact and had no obvious stains. Her dark, curly hair was cut close to her scalp and always looked neat. While many of the refugees in the room were disheveled, beaten, bloody, dirty, and looked like they'd been on the run for weeks, Sue looked competent and capable as she approached the CSS officers.

"Gentleman," Sue called out firmly as she approached the front of the room. "Can you provide an itinerary and data on our destination?" Sue stopped in front of one of the officers, directing her question to him.

For a moment, there was no response. Then the officer's fingers twitched. A moment later, he reached up slowly and grasped his big black helmet in both gloved hands and lifted it up and off of his head, revealing a shockingly thick head of light brown hair.

"Tal!" Maisy gasped, jumping to her feet.

Joanie jumped up with her and Maisy looked down at the girl, torn between the obligation to keep her safe and away from the unknown men with shocksticks and her desperate need to talk to the one person who might be able to tell her what had happened to her father.

Across the room, Tal's eyes sought out Maisy's and held her gaze. Then he looked down at Sue, who seemed tiny beside him. "We will get as much information as we can and let you know," he told her, not unkindly. The other officers turned their helmets, obviously following the conversation, but added nothing.

Tal glanced at Maisy for a long moment, turned toward the door. The unit filed out, Tal still clutching his helmet in his hands.

As the door slid shut behind them, Maisy sank back down onto the bench as Sue walked back over to their group. Joanie was still standing and hugged her mother tightly when she returned.

Still clutching Joanie to her, Sue looked down at Maisy. "You know him?" she asked.

"He was a member of my dad's crew," Maisy replied, shaking her head in confusion. "I have no idea what he's doing in that uniform." Maisy thought for a moment. "Although, the marines were all converted to CSS contracts, I guess. So maybe that makes sense? But I don't know what happened to my dad's ship, the *Sky*," she continued. "Or my dad..." Maisy trailed off.

Looking down, Maisy was overcome with exhaustion. After the stress and upheaval of the last few days...weeks...months ...She needed to crawl into a hole and have a good cry and not come out until the world made sense again. She'd known, in her bones, that her dad was dead. But now, seeing Tal here...

Pushing the thought away, Maisy walked over to the door. It opened automatically as she approached and a lone CSS officer looked back at her. She couldn't see his face through the opaque black helmet but he seemed startled.

"Can we move to the living quarters on the ship?" Maisy asked abruptly.

There was no immediate reaction. A moment passed, then two. Finally the helmeted head nodded. Maisy wondered briefly if he'd been communicating with his team lead or with the bridge but she was too tired to care.

Turning back to her group, who were all watching the byplay intently, Maisy waved them over. Joanie jumped up, pulling her mother behind her and Leo did the same. Maisy made eye contact with Lori, who seemed in a daze, and gestured again more firmly. Lori seemed to gather herself and trailed the others across the room as the rest of the refugees watched them.

Turning back to the officer, she made a guess and pointed to the right. "This way?"

Again after a brief pause, the helmet nodded. Maisy turned to the right and began trudging down the hallway, half aware of the others behind her. There were more people slowly trickling from the cafeteria, following in their wake.

They passed a medical suite with glass windows, another small cafeteria, a couple of lounges and small meeting rooms of some sort, and then they were in the crews' quarters. There were doors set a fair distance apart, suggesting the rooms were of good size, but there didn't seem to be very many of them.

It was a big ship and it was possible that there was a cryobank somewhere else but that seemed unlikely. It was obvious to Maisy that this was a freighter—and definitely not a colony ship. She'd seen plenty of recruitment vids for colony ships. This was basically a flying warehouse with an engine on one end and family quarters on the other. It was possible the freighter had been retrofitted to be a colony ship, but there were no signs of that.

This wasn't a well-funded expedition. This was a trash run.

Frowning at her own thoughts, Maisy tried the panel of the first room she passed. It opened immediately and she stepped inside. The quarters were indeed set up as a family space with a large living area with doors coming off the back wall. Walking to the doors, Maisy opened each one. There were three bedrooms and each had a private bathroom. *Swanky*, Maisy thought.

Returning to the main area of the suite, she found Lori and the others exploring the space.

"I'm too tired to look any further," Maisy declared. "This unit has three bedrooms. Lori, if you're okay sharing, I am." Lori nodded tiredly. "Then I say, let's claim this room and try to get some rest." Maisy walked over to the panel beside the door and tapped the autolock, which should prevent anyone else from entering. She walked to the large table in one corner and swung her backpack onto the surface. Reaching inside, she pulled out her last four cans of water and passed one each to Sue and Jane. "This is the last of the water, but hopefully the kitchen here works." Maisy handed the third to Lori and kept the last one for herself. She cracked the top and took a long pull.

Carrying her pack by the top strap, Maisy moved into the first bedroom. This one was slightly larger than the other two, but if she was sharing it with a toddler, she had no guilt at claiming it. Maisy dropped her bag next to the bed and lowered herself on top of the covers.

Lori hesitated in the doorway, Joey in her arms.

"It's okay," Maisy said. "Can Joey just sleep between us for now and we'll figure out a crib for him later?"

Lori nodded silently and shuffled further into the room. Maisy finally took a moment to really look at Lori and her brow furrowed in concern. Lori's vibrant hair stood out against her pale face and the dark circles under her eyes. She looked as tired as Maisy felt.

Maisy slipped off her shoes and laid back onto the pillows, watching Lori sit a sleepy Joey down on the bed. The little boy plopped over with a sigh and Maisy stroked a finger across his forehead, brushing the red fringe of his hair. The little boy's eyes closed and within moments he was breathing deeply, out for the count.

Lori lifted the cover and lowered herself onto the bed, lying on her side facing Joey.

"Goodnight," Lori said softly.

Maisy reached for her hand and squeezed it gently. Both girls stared at the sleeping boy, his rhythmic breathing lulling them to sleep.

12

Ghosts

Maisy opened her eyes and was caught by a bright blue gaze. A small, slightly sticky finger reached out and gently poked her in the eye.

"Hi, Joey." Maisy looked past the alert baby at Lori's still face, her lips slightly parted. In sleep Lori's face looked more at peace than it had the previous night.

Rolling from the bed, Maisy got to her feet and turned back to the bed to offer her hands to Joey. He didn't hesitate and lifted his arms in her direction. Maisy hefted his solid, warm weight onto her hip, slipped on her shoes, and walked quietly from the bedroom.

In the living area, Sue sat at the table, a glass of water sitting in front of her. She was gazing blankly into the distance, her thoughts a million miles away. Maisy walked over to the kitchen unit and shifted Joey to the side so she could open cabinets until she found a glass. She filled it at the tap and held it to the light, satisfied it looked potable.

She was taking nothing for granted at this point. Continuing to open cabinets, she found a box of protein bars, cereal, boxes of shelf-stable milk, and stasis-sealed bread. The cooler was empty but functional.

Grabbing two protein bars, Maisy made her way back to the table, sitting across from Sue but not interrupting her reverie. Positioning Joey on her lap, Maisy helped the little boy take a drink of the water, then broke off pieces of protein bar and watched him carefully as he chewed them. Maisy looked up to find Sue's gaze on her.

"Thank you," Sue said.

Maisy cocked her head in confusion. "For what?"

"For sticking with Joanie," Sue explained. "I can't imagine what might have happened to her if she'd been on her own." Sue visibly shuddered, her eyes haunted by what could have been.

"I wouldn't have left her," Maisy said, "but you're totally underestimating your kid. She would have been okay no matter what." Maisy smiled.

Sitting on her lap, Joey smiled too and reached up to pat Maisy's face. "Poop," he said clearly.

Crap, thought Maisy. Like a deer in headlights, she froze in the face of mortal danger.

Across the table Sue burst out laughing. She stood up from the table and walked around to Maisy's side, extending her arms to Joey. "I've got this one, Maze," Sue said, still laughing. Joey reached up to her and Sue scooped him into her arms, whisking him away to do her magic.

Maisy breathed a sigh of relief and finished her protein bar in peace. Taking in the unit after several hours of sleep Maisy looked around and noticed several personal items. Standing from the table, she approached a group of photocells hung on the wall behind the table. Most were scenes from Earth's landscape but there were two that showed what looked like family units, arms around each other's shoulders.

Turning to take in the rest of the unit, Maisy noted the pretty patterned pillows on the bench and the flowered glassware in the cabinets. These weren't standard issue items.

Walking quietly back into the bedroom, Maisy glanced at the still sleeping Lori and circled the bed to open the storage unit built into the wall. She wasn't surprised to find it full of clothes. Pulling out the drawers below, she found more clothing, a stack of personal documents, a handful of books, and a tablet.

Scooping up the tablet, Maisy silently closed everything back up and made her way back out to the main area. Reclaiming her seat at the table, Maisy thumbed on the tablet, relieved to see it still had battery and noted that it was almost noon by ship's time. Scrolling through the apps, she found several diagnostic programs.

Clicking on the first one, Maisy leaned closer to the tablet. The screen was displaying the current status of the *Oro Zapato II*. And it was not good. There were yellow and red lights across the board.

Every system was compromised.

Flipping to a graphic view of the data, there was a clear pattern of damage across the back of the ship. Half of the engines were gone. There were three cargo bays on the ship like the one they'd been dumped in and two of them were open to space. There were breaches in several compartments and life support was running at forty percent capacity.

Awesome, Maisy thought. She laid the tablet down and rested her forehead in her hands, eyes closed. Joanie and Sue didn't deserve this. None of them did.

Maisy sat there quietly, not moving, until Sue came back into the room accompanied by a chattering Joanie and cooing Joey. Maisy pressed her hands into her eyes for a moment, then wiped them hard, scrubbing at her face. Sue's hand landed softly on her shoulder and Maisy took a deep breath before looking up with a twisted smile.

"I've got some bad news," Maisy told the older woman.

"Can it wait until after breakfast?" Sue asked.

"Yes, absolutely." Maisy's smile turned a little more genuine and she gladly accepted the clean baby Sue deposited onto her lap.

A frantic Lori appeared in the doorway to the left bedroom. Her eyes found Joey and her body sagged in relief. She stood there for a moment, clutching the doorframe. Maisy didn't say anything, giving the other girl a moment to recover.

"Can you keep watching him for a moment?" she asked.

"Sure. Take your time," Maisy replied. "We'll be right here."

Lori nodded and made a valiant attempt at a smile before ducking back into the bedroom. When she came back out a couple of minutes later she looked much better. She'd brushed her hair and looked awake and ready to face the challenges of the new day. Maisy was suddenly aware that she had skipped her morning routine for several days in a row and was less than fresh.

Standing, she handed Joey over to Lori's waiting arms. "My turn."

A few minutes later, Maisy emerged from the bath wrapped in one of the towels she'd found and rifled through the clothes in the room's cabinet. Grabbing black pants and a black t-shirt, Maisy pulled her damp, curly hair into a loose bun and headed back into the main room.

Leo and his mom had joined the group at the table and everyone was eating. The abandoned tablet was still sitting in front of her empty chair, but now a bowl and glass of water sat beside it.

Sliding back into the seat, Maisy picked up one of the boxes of cereal from the center of the table and filled the bowl, adding milk. Everyone ate in silence, but an air of anticipation filled the room as if everyone was waiting for the other shoe to drop.

As Maisy spooned the last of the milk from her bowl into her mouth, Joanie appeared by her elbow. The little girl smiled as she took Maisy's dishes over to the kitchen unit. Around the table, Leo and Jane were talking quietly to each other while Sue cooed at Joey. The remnants of his second breakfast decorated his face and Sue was carefully cleaning him up as Lori watched. When Joanie came back to the table, she slipped back into the seat on Lori's other side, trying to get Joey's attention.

"Maisy has some news," Sue announced and Maisy started. She'd almost forgotten, lost in the quiet peace of this little scene of domesticity.

"I found this tablet in the bedroom," Maisy gestured to the device sitting on the table. "There were also clothes and personal effects left behind. It looks like this belonged to an engineer because it's loaded with all kinds of diagnostic apps." Maisy hesitated, not sure how to continue.

"Diagnostics for the ship?" Jane asked.

Maisy nodded and Jane reached for the tablet. She quickly thumbed through to the screen Maisy had been looking at, obviously familiar with the app. "Well, crap," Jane said.

"Yeah," Maisy concurred.

"What?" asked Sue, concerned. She looked back and forth between the two of them, her brow furrowed. Jane was scrolling through the data intently, so Maisy answered.

"This ship has been all shot to hell," she said baldly. Jane didn't look up but nodded in agreement. "Half of the systems are flashing red and the environmental systems are at less than half of capacity." Thinking of how long the systems would hold out, Maisy had a thought. "Jane, do you see any nav data? Anything about our destination?"

Shaking her head, Jane replied, "I don't see anything, but I'll keep looking. The good news is that we're topped up on fuel."

"Colony ship, my ass," Sue said.

"Yeah, this is definitely a freighter," Maisy agreed. "Or it was. Now it's the bits and pieces of one barely being held together. Our destination better not be too far..." There were looks of horror on the faces around her and Maisy trailed off.

Oops, she thought. *That may have been too much honesty.*

Pushing her chair back from the table, Maisy announced, "I'm going to see if I can find that guy I know and get any more info. I'll be back as soon as I can."

Jane was still engrossed in the tablet, but Sue and Lori shared a look of concern. Joanie and Leo were playing some kind of game and never looked up. Taking that as her cue, Maisy made her exit.

At the door of the unit she hesitated, feeling naked without her bag, but decided against going back into the bedroom for it. At this point, there was nothing in there that could make a difference. She wondered for a moment if she could clone the permissions of the tablet she'd found to gain access to the ship's network on her own tablet, and made a mental note to try when she returned.

Maisy's memories from yesterday were a blur. She'd been so physically and emotionally exhausted that the ship's hallways seemed only vaguely familiar. She was mildly surprised that there were no CSS officers stationed in the corridors and wondered how many had been left on the ship.

Maisy had a general idea of the ship's layout from the map she'd found on the tablet. Her first stop was the cafeteria they'd all congregated in after the massacre in the cargo bay.

The doors slid open as she approached and Maisy was relieved to see signs of life. The food processors on the far wall seemed to be working and people sat scattered throughout the tables, mostly in small groups. It was quiet and conversations were hushed. Everyone seemed subdued but they were in much better shape. It looked like everyone had access to showers and clean clothes at least.

Walking over to the bank of food processors, Maisy scrolled through the options on the panel and selected a flavored protein bar. Receiving her selection, she turned back to the room.

When she scanned the occupants around her, she didn't see anyone she knew, although there were several familiar faces that she recognized from yesterday. The woman she'd seen yesterday with a broken arm was now sporting a transparent plasti-cast. She considered approaching her or one of the others to see if there was any new information but decided to go in search of it firsthand.

Taking bites of her protein bar, Maisy made her way back out of the cafeteria and into the hallway. She hadn't seen the direction Tal had taken yesterday, but the bridge was a good place to start.

In theory the bridge should be directly above the crew quarters, so Maisy headed left, looking for the elevator to get to the next level. It was generally where she expected it to be, but she was still surprised to encounter no guards. The elevator opened automatically as she approached and the panel accepted her commands. The car began moving upward easily and a moment later the doors opened on the bridge deck.

Finishing her bar and brushing her hands against her borrowed pants, Maisy stepped cautiously from the car. She was shocked that there were no officers stationed in the hallway outside of the bridge either.

Approaching the door cautiously, Maisy moved just close enough to trigger the sensor and took a half step back. No one came storming out. There were no shocksticks or black helmets to be found. She leaned forward gingerly until she could see onto the bridge.

There were six uniformed CSS officers on the bridge, none of them wearing helmets. Tal stood at a station near the door, his back toward Maisy. Next to him stood Joe. A man with close cut salt and pepper hair sat in the captain's chair talking to a young woman with dark hair and deep olive skin. On the other side of the bridge, a tall older woman with short, spiky blond hair and another older man stood at stations, engrossed in their work.

The captain glanced over at Maisy as she leaned her head into the room. "Who the hell are you?" he barked at her. Tal whipped around, his eyes going wide when he recognized her.

Turning to the captain, Tal said, "Captain Tratt, this is Jackson Renner's daughter, Maisy. She was among the...*colonists.*" Maisy noted his hesitation. "I'll escort her back to quarters."

"And set some security on the damn elevators. The *colonists* should be restricted to the crew quarters." The captain threw Maisy an irritated glance before dismissing her and resuming his conversation.

Tal moved quickly toward the hatch, grabbing Maisy's arm and manhandling her back toward the elevator. The doors opened and Tal dragged her inside, spinning them around to face the panel. As he reached out to tap the level with his left hand Maisy wrenched her arm from his, rounding on him in anger.

"What the hell?" Maisy started, ready to rip into him. He turned to face the oncoming tirade and Maisy stopped as she looked at his face. She'd been too tired yesterday and too surprised by his presence to really process what she was seeing.

Now, looking at Tal with fresh eyes, Maisy was shocked. His face had new lines in the...week?...since she'd last seen him. Deep shadows were carved out under his cheekbones and his eyes were sunken into his skull. As Maisy watched, his face collapsed and he brought his hands up to cover his haunted eyes.

Her heart aching, Maisy reached out and wrapped her hand around his wrist. "What happened?" she said quietly. The elevator door slid open but they both ignored it. Tal lowered his hands from his face, slipping his wrist from her grasp and turning his palm to capture her hand instead. He met her gaze with an intensity that hurt and Maisy began shaking her head before he even started speaking.

"The *Sky* is gone, Maisy. Joe and I were the only ones who made it off."

Maisy looked up at the ceiling, holding her eyes wide. She'd known, but she hadn't let herself think about it. There'd been too much else going on and she'd been focused on helping the others, so she hadn't had to think about her dad.

Still shaking her head, Maisy asked again, her voice barely above a whisper, "What happened?"

Tal grabbed her other hand as well, enveloping both of her hands in his. He took a deep, trembling breath that rattled through his chest, where their hands pressed. "There was a distress call. This ship, the *Oro*, was being attacked by pirates." Tal swallowed, closing his eyes.

"There was a fire. Jackson sent Joe and I down to engineering to put it out. When the abandon ship alarm went off I couldn't believe it. We'd gotten the fire out and we were on the stairs, heading back to the bridge." Tal's eyes were squeezed shut tight but tears still leaked out.

"But Jackson said to go. The reactor was blowing." Tal's eyes opened and he gazed down into Maisy's face. "So we left. I'm so sorry, Maisy. I thought he was right behind me. That they all were."

The tears were flowing now and Tal's voice was thick.

"The ship blew and none of the other pods had launched. I'm so sorry."

Maisy pulled her hands from Tal's and reached up to wrap her arms around his shoulder. He was tall but his shoulders still had the narrowness of youth and they shook with his sobs. Tal bent down and buried his head in her shoulder, wrapping his arms around her waist.

Maisy rested her hand against the back of his head, her fingers sinking into his thick hair. It was softer than she had imagined it would be.

"Thank you," she whispered. "Thank you for telling me. I knew he was gone, but I needed to know what happened."

Maisy's own tears finally overflowed and she leaned her forehead into Tal's collarbone and the two of them just stood in the glaring lights of the elevator and held onto each other and cried.

13

Ship of fools

Maisy walked quickly through the halls of the ship, backtracking once but finally making her way back to the crew quarters. Tapping the panel, she remembered they'd locked the door from the inside, so she knocked and waited. A moment later the door slid open to reveal Sue, who relaxed visibly when she saw Maisy.

"Oh, thank god," Sue said, pulling Maisy into the unit and into her arms.

This is a lot of hugging, Maisy thought as the door slid shut behind her.

"I'm ok," Maisy told the older woman, patting her back awkwardly.

"We were so worried!" Sue exclaimed, pulling back to grip Maisy by her shoulders and examine her face. Maisy knew she would see evidence of her recent tears.

"I found out what happened to my dad," Maisy explained briefly. She swallowed, closing her eyes briefly. "He didn't make it."

Sue pulled Maisy back in for another hug, firmer and longer than the last one. A small force crashed against Maisy's right hip and she reached down to pull Joanie against her. From her other side, Leo wrapped his arms around her waist more gently. A second later, hands touched her back, a head resting on her shoulder. Jane and Lori.

Maisy didn't want to cry again, but tears ran down her face. After a moment she pulled back and reached up to scrub them away.

"I'm ok," she repeated. "Thank you, guys." Maisy looked at the three women standing around her. "Let's sit down and I'll tell you what I found out."

Maisy walked over to the kitchen and grabbed a glass of water before crossing to the table and taking the seat she'd been in earlier. Joanie and Leo sat on the floor in the corner where Joey had a makeshift fort set up, playing quietly with the baby. Sue, Lori, and Jane joined Maisy at the table, each looking at her expectantly.

Maisy nodded to Jane. "We were right, this ship was all shot to hell. They were attacked by pirates. My dad's ship, the *Sky*, responded to their distress call. The *Oro* got away, but my dad's ship didn't make it. Tal and another crewmember made it off." Maisy paused and took a deep breath. "Tal said, when they were picked up and brought back to the station, they were put into this new unit. He doesn't seem crazy about it. But they're the only ones on the ship. Just six of them."

Jane looked up in shock. That was well short of a full crew.

"Did he say where we're going?" Sue asked.

"The planet is in sector 12, number 761, which means nothing to me. He said he'd see if he could find out more information on it." Maisy sighed. "But here's the really bad news. It's far. Like, really far. It's going to take us a solid year to get there, assuming we don't have any issues—which, with the ship having huge holes in it, seems unlikely."

"There has to be a cryobank on board," Sue said.

"There is...but it only has thirty units. And there are way more people than that on board right now," Maisy replied. "And that's another issue. There's no official manifest. The crew doesn't even have a list of the people on board. This was not well-planned."

"It's a write-off," Sue said. The other three women looked at her and Sue continued. "This ship was probably leased from Citatech. When a corp loses a big piece of equipment they can either put the money into it to repair it or they can submit it as a total loss and get a payout for the book value. Then they can either cannibalize it for parts or scuttle it. Whichever is easier."

Maisy grimaced. "So our little colony is their way of scuttling the ship and getting rid of a bunch of troublemakers all at the same time. Awesome."

Jane nodded. "It makes sense. Station management wanted to boost output, so they needed to cull the population and clear the lower decks. They probably ran a cost-benefit ratio and targeted low-output workers, then swept up anyone else who made waves. No consolidated government to complain to anymore, so they could just do what tracked for their bottom line."

"That makes sense," Sue agreed. "Who needs a compliance officer when you've decided not to be compliant."

"Or a safety engineer," Jane said.

"My parents were probably top of their list," added Lori. "The union cost them time and money, insisting on better pay, time off, safety regs." Lori gave a small, sad smile. "Anyone who ever met my mom for two minutes would have realized she didn't have a mute button. There was no way they were going to get her to shut up..." Lori trailed off, her eyes far away.

Sitting next to Lori, Sue reached over and covered her hand with her own, giving it a gentle squeeze.

Suddenly, the lights in the unit dimmed.

"Ship's night," Jane announced quickly, the tension in the room spiking. "It's okay. It's normal."

The others calmed down quickly, but hearts still beat a little too fast. It was normal for ships to automatically lower their lights at predetermined times. Usually lowering to seventy percent, then forty percent about an hour later. It helped to sync crew and passenger circadian rhythms and lower energy usage.

Lori stood from the table and walked over to Joey's makeshift crib where the little boy was cuddled against Joanie, the two fast asleep. Leo sat next to them, only half awake. Lori carefully lifted Joey from Joanie's embrace and carried the little boy into the first bedroom. Jane walked over to the sleepy Leo and held out her hand, pulling him to his feet. The two walked quietly into the third bedroom.

Maisy looked expectantly at Sue but she shook her head.

"I'm not tired at all," she said. "I'm going to stay up for a bit, maybe look through this tablet." Sue gestured to the tablet Jane had left on the table.

"I have my tablet in my bag. I'll see if I can clone the settings on this one and get into the network." Maisy jumped up from the table with purpose but hesitated at the door to the first bedroom. Knocking softly, she stood awkwardly, listening for movement within.

"Come in," Lori called, in a normal voice.

Maisy tapped the panel beside the door and it slid open. At her quizzical look, Lori explained, "Joey isn't a light sleeper. At all." Lori smiled a small, sad smile as she looked down at the baby, snuggled into another makeshift containment area against the bedroom wall. "My parents were not quiet people. Joey could sleep through a nuclear blast."

"Good to know," Maisy said, returning the smile. She crossed to the left side of the bed, where she'd left her bag, and pulled out her tablet. "I'm going to see if I can get access to the ship's network."

"Good luck," Lori said. "Don't let me touch it, I'm death to technology." She rolled her eyes at herself.

"Also good to know!" Maisy laughed, moving back around the bed toward the door of the room. Lori met her there, reaching out to stop her with a gentle hand on her arm. Maisy's smile faded, knowing what was coming.

"I'm sorry about your dad," Lori said softly.

"I'm sorry about your parents, too," Maisy replied, determined not to cry again.

"Thank you, Maisy," Lori said intently. "Thank you for helping me, for helping us. Yesterday is a blur but I know you didn't leave us. Thank you."

Maisy put her hand over Lori's on her arm for a moment. "We'll be okay. We all just need to stick together." The girls moved apart, both swallowing back tears.

Maisy left the room quickly and made her way back to the table, tablet in hand. Sue was still sitting there, tapping at the other device. Maisy sat across from her and accessed the settings on her tablet, scanning for nearby devices.

Immediately the other machine ID popped up. Just like there was no security on the input, the net connection also was completely open. *Sloppy*, thought Maisy. This ship must have never taken on any paying passengers. Only a closed family ship would be so lax with security.

Pulling up a utility app on her tablet Maisy was able to initiate the clone. "You should see a prompt," she told Sue.

"Got it. Accept?"

"Yes, please." A second later data was flowing into her tablet. "Cool." Maisy looked up at Sue. "I have an idea."

The next morning, Maisy was sitting at the table with a glass of water, tapping on her tablet, when Lori emerged from the bedroom. The trauma of the last few days had left their mark, but her hair was freshly washed and her eyes bright.

"Joey is still sleeping," she said by way of greeting, walking over to the kitchen to grab a glass of water for herself. "You weren't up all night, were you?" she asked, frowning.

"Nope. I haven't been up that long." Maisy looked up at Lori, arching one brow. "Joey isn't the only one who sleeps like the dead."

Lori barked out a laugh, walking back to the table with her glass.

"We need to get more food today," Lori said. "I've got enough for breakfast and lunch for Joey but that's it."

"As soon as everyone is up we'll make a run to the cafeteria," Maisy replied. "It's time we try to get organized, and that's the best place to do it."

"Organized?" Lori echoed warily.

"We need to know how many people are on board, and who they are. We need to explore the ship and find any other tablets or pads so that we can communicate with each other. If we're going to be on this ship for the foreseeable future, we need a plan."

"It's a little early in the morning for all of that," Lori protested. "And shouldn't the CSS be doing that?"

"Probably," Maisy agreed. "But it doesn't look like they are. There are only six of them and they're not a real unit."

"Great," Lori sighed. "I need coffee." Just like that she sounded exhausted again. Rising from the table she crossed to the small kitchen unit and began rifling the cabinets for a source of caffeine. She was still on the hunt when the center bedroom opened and Joanie stepped out. The little girl was wearing a borrowed shirt several sizes too big, the shirtsleeves rolled up and the hem past her knees.

"Maze!" Joanie called out. "My mom is still asleep. Can you make me some cereal?"

"I can," replied Maisy, getting to her feet.

"I think we finished the milk last night," Lori cautioned.

"Then I guess it's time for that cafeteria run." Maisy grabbed her black bag from the back of her chair and swung it onto her shoulder.

"I'll go with you," Lori said quickly.

Maisy paused by the door. "What if Joey wakes up?"

"I can watch him!" Joanie offered.

Sue stepped from the middle bedroom at that moment, taking in the scene at a glance. "And I'll watch her," she added, smiling at the older girls. "Be careful. And take your time."

Lori smiled in gratitude and the two girls slipped from the suite, making sure the door closed behind them.

"Getting cabin fever?" Maisy asked as they walked down the hall, shoulder to shoulder.

"Maybe a little," Lori answered. "My emotions are all over the place. It's just good to have something concrete to do."

Maisy nodded, understanding.

Lori tilted her head toward Maisy. "You seem...ok?" Lori let the question hang.

"I'm not," Maisy shrugged. Pulling her tablet from her bag, she tapped through to the app she'd downloaded from the network last night and tilted the screen to show Lori.

"How about a scavenger hunt to take our minds off of things for a little while?" she asked Lori with a mischievous smile.

Lori looked at the flashing dots scattered around the ship's map. "A scavenger hunt? For what?"

"For tablets, mostly," Maisy explained. "There are a couple of wrist units and a couple of devices I didn't recognize, but all of these ULIs are devices connected to the network." Maisy turned left down the corridor, away from the cafeteria. "If we can collect these devices and distribute them among the *colonists* then we'll have better access and a way to communicate with each other."

"A way to *organize*," Lori said, smiling. "My mom would have absolutely approved. I'm in." Lori thought for a moment. "But Joanie is waiting for milk for her cereal, so let's not be too long?"

"We'll just check the two on this corridor." She tapped the panel on the first door and it slid open automatically, revealing an empty room. This unit was much smaller than the one they were in currently, but about twice the size of the one she'd shared with her dad on the station.

Following the Universal Location Indicator signal displayed on her tablet, Maisy crossed to a storage unit beside the bunk in the corner of the room. Pulling open drawers, she pulled out a tablet similar to the one they'd found in the other room. She dumped it in her bag and they moved quickly back into the hall where Lori stood fidgeting by the doorway.

Further down the corridor, Maisy tried the next door, but this time, it stayed closed. She exchanged a glance with Lori before knocking softly. The panel slid open to reveal a man with a full beard. He stared at the two girls suspiciously from bruised eyes.

"Who is it, Sean?" called a woman's voice from behind him. Maisy shifted slightly to gaze past the man to see the woman with the broken arm, sitting on a padded bench.

"Can we come in?" asked Maisy, addressing the woman.

The man glanced back at the woman with the broken arm and she nodded. He stepped back, allowing the girls to enter. Maisy followed the indicator on her tablet to the kitchen unit on the wall opposite the woman. Lori stayed at the door while Maisy pulled open cabinets.

"What are you looking for?" the woman asked.

Maisy pulled a small mini tablet from a drawer and held it aloft. "This."

Maisy walked over to the woman's side and sat next to her on the bench. Thumbing the tablet awake, she found a rudimentary password. Setting the mini on the bench between them, Maisy tapped her own tablet several times, accessing the device through the network and disabling the security. Maisy switched back to the mini and this time was able to access all of its apps with no prompt.

Scrolling quickly through the list, Maisy saw that it held a subset of what they'd found on the other machine. Opening a simple bulletin board app, Maisy handed the device to the woman.

"You can access the ship's network with this now. I'm Maisy. I posted this announcement asking people to meet at the cafeteria at 1800 hours. This is Lori," Maisy added as Lori trailed the man over. He sat on the woman's other side, peering over her shoulder at the mini.

Maisy rose from the bench and moved quickly back toward the door of the unit, Lori following her out.

"Thank you!" the woman called after them.

"See you tonight." Maisy waved as she slipped through the door. In the hallway, she shared a smile of accomplishment with Lori as they headed back toward the cafeteria.

"Food?" Lori asked.

"Food," Maisy agreed.

In the cafeteria, there was a teenage boy sitting alone and two other small groups. While Lori accessed the food processors built into the wall, Maisy approached each of the groups and let them know they'd be meeting there that evening. Lori joined her as she walked up to the last table. A gangly boy about Maisy's age looked up at them warily as they approached.

"I'm Maisy and this is Lori. We're asking everyone to meet back here in about eight hours." Maisy realized the boy still had a wrist unit. "Have you been able to access the ship's network with your wrist unit?"

He shook his head mutely, barely pausing from eating his cereal.

"If you let me see it, I may be able to fix that." Maisy stood quietly beside the table, waiting for the boy to make up his mind.

After a second, he paused in his eating, letting his spoon rest in the bowl, and removed the unit from his wrist. He sat it on the table and slid it across. Maisy took a seat opposite the boy and pulled her tablet from her bag. She quickly cloned her access codes and passed them to the wrist unit. Slipping her tablet back into her bag, she picked up the wrist unit and accepted the prompt.

"There you go," she said. "We're meeting here at 1800, ship's time." She rose from the table and turned to Lori, whose arms were full of food. Offloading half of her burden onto Maisy, Lori led the way back to their suite.

Sue opened the door immediately when they knocked and Joanie let out a cheer from behind her at the sight of their haul. An alert and happy Joey sat her on lap, picking dry cereal bits from the table across from Leo. Jane poked her head out of the third bedroom at the noise, smiling at the girls.

"We were only a little worried," Jane said with a shrug.

"We found two more tablets. We left one with some people and brought the other with us. I also hooked up a guy's wrist unit," Maisy reported as she and Lori began unloading food onto the countertop in the kitchen.

"Do you still want a bowl of cereal, Joanie?" Lori asked. At the little girl's enthusiastic affirmative, Lori brought one of the milk canisters they'd retrieved from the cafeteria over to the table. "How about you, Leo?"

"Yes, please," the little boy said politely.

Lori brought them over two bowls and spoons, lifting Joey from Joanie's lap.

"He's been changed and fed," Sue said. "He's such a happy baby. Joanie loves playing with him."

"Thank you." Lori smiled. "Both of you." She reached out a hand and touched Joanie's head, smiling gratefully at the little girl, who waved her spoon at her in acknowledgement, her mouth already full of cereal and milk.

Lori sat at the table, cradling Joey, and Maisy sat across from her, taking both her own and the new tablet out of her bag and setting them on the table before her. The new device, like the one they'd found in this room, had no security, not even a rudimentary password.

Shrugging at the sloppy digital hygiene of people she'd never meet, Maisy scrolled through the apps to see if there was any info they hadn't already had access to. Seeing nothing, she slid the tablet back into her bag.

"I'm going to head back out and see if I can pick up some more devices. So far, we've got two others floating out there. I'll pass this one onto another group too if I get the chance." Maisy stood and moved toward the door of the unit and Sue got to her feet as well.

"I'll go with you this time," she said firmly. "Lori, are you okay to keep an eye on Joanie for a little while?"

"Of course," Lori said. "We'll be fine. Good luck keeping Maisy out of trouble." The two shared a look as Maisy rolled her eyes at them.

Exiting an empty unit an hour later, Maisy slipped the tablet they'd recovered into her bag and headed back the way they'd come.

"Looks like there's one more device on this hall," she said to Sue.

This time the door didn't open, indicating the unit was occupied. Maisy and Sue exchanged a glance, then Maisy gently knocked on the door. A moment later, it slid open to reveal a middle aged man with a wary expression.

"We're tracking network devices. There's a tablet in this room. Can we come in and look for it?" Maisy asked.

The man hesitated, glancing over his shoulder. Behind him, another older man and a young boy were sitting at a table.

"Come in, " the man said, moving back from the doorway. "A tablet? With access to the ship's network?"

"Yes, " Maisy answered, following the signal on her own tablet to a drawer built into one of the benches. Pulling out the tablet, she handed it to the man. He tried to open the apps but was blocked by a biometric prompt.

"Hold on." In less than a minute, she had removed the security and unlocked the device.

She handed the tablet back to him. "There you go. You now have access to the network. If you check out the board, we've started a thread to help us communicate and get organized. We're going to meet at 1800 hours in the cafeteria, if you'd like to join us."

He glanced up at Maisy, looking bemused. "We'll be there."

Maisy nodded and gestured for Sue to proceed her from the unit. In the hallway, they turned to the left to head back to their suite.

"Another kid."

Sue nodded. "Maybe five or six years old." She sighed, shaking her head. "Those bastards on the station should be shot."

"You're not wrong," Maisy said. "But the important thing right now is figuring out a plan."

Sue was silent for a moment, deep in thought. As the two rounded a corner, they nearly collided with a black-uni-formed CSS officer.

"Tal!" Maisy cried in relief.

Sue looked over at her. "This is one of the marines who served with your dad?" she asked.

"Yes, this is Tal. Tal, this is my friend, Sue. She and her daughter were our neighbors on the station."

"Nice to meet you, Sue," Tal replied politely. "Can I borrow Maze, for just a moment?"

Maisy swung her backpack off her shoulder and handed it to Sue. "I'll meet you back at the room. Can you give that to Jane?"

Sue accepted the bag, nodding. "Don't be long, okay?"

"I won't," Maisy reassured her.

Sue took a long look at Tal, frowning a little in concern, but continued down the hall, disappearing around the next corner.

Maisy stood awkwardly in front of Tal, trying hard not to remember their last encounter.

"How are you doing?" Tal asked. "I meant to ask where you're staying."

"We're in the first room in corridor D, the one that leads from the cafeteria to the crew quarters section. There is a group of us sharing."

"That's good. I'm glad you're sticking together," Tal said earnestly. "I'm glad you're not alone."

"Me too." Maisy sighed, not wanting to go there again. "How are you doing? With the new unit?" she asked, changing the topic.

"Honestly, it's not going well." Tal frowned, rubbing his long, tapered fingers against his forehead.

"With the new captain?" Maisy wasn't surprised.

"Yeah," he said, shaking his head. "Maybe I was just spoiled with your dad, you know?" Tal looked up and met Maisy's eyes. "I know I'm green, but Jackson never treated me like a kid." Tal gave a watery laugh, pulling a hand over his face. "He called me *kid*, but it never felt like an insult. Captain Tratt..." Tal trailed off.

"None of us want to be here. I get that. But we're still marines." Tal's lips twisted and he scrubbed at his face. "Or maybe we're not."

Maisy let the silence sit awkwardly between them for a moment, waiting to see if Tal would explain more of the issues on the bridge. When he didn't seem inclined to elaborate, she prompted him gently, "What did you want to talk to me about?"

"Are you getting what you need for the baby?" Tal asked. Maisy pulled back from him in surprise.

"How did you know we have a baby in our group?"

"I saw you...on the station." Tal hesitated. "I was the one who dropped off the food when you guys were on H deck." He looked at her sheepishly, while Maisy's mouth hung open in shock.

"Oh my god," she said, when she could finally speak. "I had no idea that was you. Thank you!" Maisy wanted to hug him, but there's been a lot of that going on lately. "Really, thank you. That made such a huge difference."

Tal shrugged off her thanks, looking uncomfortable. "So are you guys okay with what's available from the processors in the cafe?"

"Yes, it's been fine." Maisy hesitated, considering her options. "We've been asking the people on board to meet in the cafeteria at 1800 tonight," she told him. "So we can get a head count, and get to know each other."

Maisy watched Tal's reaction, wondering how much she should trust him. "We know we're going to be on this ship for a while."

"Yeah." Tal agreed, looking torn. "This isn't a good situation, Maze. I'm not sure how much I'm allowed to tell you...." Tal looked over his shoulder, as if expecting his new captain to be standing behind him with a disapproving look on his face. Turning back to Maisy, Tal reached for her hand. "Let me talk to the others. I'll try to come tonight, okay?"

Maisy nodded, watching silently as he turned away and hurried back down the corridor toward the elevator. Forcing herself to move, Maisy turned in the opposite direction and headed back toward her suite. She wondered what aspect of their current situation Tal was worried about. There were so many options to choose from.

By the time 1800 rolled around, Maisy and Jane had unlocked all of the tablets that they had been able to recover and had also figured out how to use Maisy's tablet to lock and unlock the suite door. This meant that all of them could go to the meeting without either leaving their new suite unlocked or leaving someone behind to let them back in. So at a couple of minutes before 1800, Maisy was walking down the hall toward the cafeteria behind Joanie and Leo, Sue and Jane leading the way up ahead, and Lori walking at her side with Joey in her arms. Maisy had her black bag slung over her shoulder, full of unlocked devices.

She had spoken to several groups, both in the cafeteria throughout the day and also in the units she'd visited on her scavenger hunt, but she was still shocked to see how many had actually shown up. This seemed like the majority of the colonists—or refugees—based on what she recalled from their arrival. They were seated in groups of various sizes at the benches across the cafeteria. There were hushed conversations here and there but for the most part, it was eerily quiet. Maisy scanned the room for Tal, but didn't see him.

Jane and Sue led the group to an empty table and everyone sat except Maisy, who walked to the next table. Recognizing one of the men at the table, she nodded at the tablet in his hands.

Moving to the next table Maisy didn't see any familiar faces.

"Does anyone have a device?" she asked. "A tablet or a wrist unit?"

The members of the group looked at each other, no one responding. Maisy pulled one of the mini tablets from her bag and handed it to the woman to her left.

"Now you do. We're using the board app to communicate for now. It's not sophisticated but it's better than nothing."

The woman took the tablet, her eyes wide. "Thank you.".

Maisy nodded and moved to the next table. By this point, everyone was watching her progress and following along. The conversations throughout the cafeteria had gotten louder, but at least everyone seemed patient and content to wait while Maisy moved through the room. The next table was able to produce their own device. Maisy waved Jane over and the older woman came over to the table and used Maisy's tablet to get their device access to the network. Maisy moved onto the next table.

They ran out of devices before they ran out of tables but in the end, only two groups left empty-handed. "We'll find devices for everyone so you can stay in touch. Give me a couple of days to keep searching the ship, okay?" The men and women around the table nodded.

The last table held the two men and the boy they'd met yesterday.

"You guys are all set?" Maisy asked.

The older man nodded.

Maisy caught the gaze of the boy, "Are you okay?"

The boy glanced at the man, who nodded. The boy turned back to Maisy and nodded.

"You're welcome to come and visit with us if you want," Maisy told him, gesturing to her table and the kids seated there. He seemed to look longingly in their direction but he didn't respond, so Maisy decided to leave it for the moment.

"My name is Maisy and I'm in the first room down the hall."

"My name is Ted," the little boy said quietly.

"If you ever need anything, just come and find me. Okay?"

The little boy nodded again and gave Maisy a small smile.

Turning back to the room, Maisy scanned the people seated there. Sue's task had been to try to log how many people were present and get an idea of the groups. It would be interesting to see what the final headcount was.

"Thank you, everyone, for coming. For the next couple of days, we're going to meet here every day at 1800 to give people a chance to communicate. Everyone is welcome. If there's something you need, please let us know and we'll figure it out. There's food here and clothes in the units."

People had started filing out when a man stood and called out, "Who's in charge here?" The people walking out paused, looking around. The man was middle-aged, with thinning brown hair and a slight pouch, accentuated by unflattering coveralls. He looked around expectantly but no one responded.

"There's a CSS unit on board, and they're in charge. But I don't think we're their top priority at the moment." Maisy replied matter-of-factly. "I think we're on our own." There were nods of agreement and the refugees by the door started moving again.

Maisy had turned back to her group when a commotion near the door drew her attention. Tal walked in, still in uniform but without his helmet. It was obvious that many of the others were caught off guard. They'd all had some traumatic encounters with the CSS in the past week or so, and they gave him a very wide berth.

By the time Tal had crossed the room to Maisy's table, the rest of the cafeteria had cleared out. He came to stand at her side and Maisy turned to her group, still seated around the table. "This is Tal, who was a member of my dad's crew."

"But he's CSS now," Lori said, her voice flat.

"Not by choice," Tal said. Maisy looked at him, surprised by the vehemence in his voice.

"Tal is the one who brought us the food when we were on the station," Maisy told Lori gently. Lori's eyes flashed back to Tal, seeming to take in his height and make a mental comparison. Finally, she nodded, warmth returning to her face.

Maisy turned back to Tal. "Has something changed?" she asked. "You don't look happy."

Tal shook his head. "This isn't a good situation for any of us. No one is happy."

"Well, that's true," Jane interjected.

Reminded of introductions, Maisy said, "Tal, this is Jane and her son Leo." Jane and Tal exchanged nods. "You met Sue. This is her daughter Joanie." Tal smiled at Joanie, who gave him a little wave. "And this is Lori and her little brother, Joey. Thank you again for watching out for us back on the station."

Tal waved Maisy's thanks away, frowning. "It was the only thing I could do to try to make things better." Tal sighed. "What a mess."

"Sit down," Maisy said firmly.

Tal folded his tall frame into the bench seat of the table and Maisy sat beside him.

"What's going on now?" Maisy probed again.

Tal looked torn, but he'd come down to the cafeteria to meet with them, so she was fairly sure he'd share the information he had. "Did you tell them about the planet?"

"What you'd told me, yes." Maisy answered. "That it was in sector 12 and it'll take us a year to get there."

"And we don't have enough cryo units for everyone?"

"Yeah. So is there a plan?"

"No...or at least not a good one," Tal scrubbed his hands down his face in a mixture of exhaustion and frustration. "Tratt is suggesting some pretty radical options. So far we've been able to talk him down, but..." Tal trailed off.

"What kind of options?" Sue asked suspiciously.

Tal met her gaze. "The kind of options that only require thirty cryo units. Or the kind of options that don't require going to the planet...because there are no colonists left to drop off."

Maisy inhaled sharply and Tal turned to look at her. Maisy's hand was fisted on the tabletop and Tal reached out to cover it.

"I won't let that happen," he said firmly.

"No one would care," Jane pointed out. "Back on the station, I mean. He would return a hero for saving all that time and fuel. This whole *colony* thing was just an excuse to get rid of the remainder of the riff raff."

"What Tratt doesn't realize—or won't let himself admit—is that as far as Citatech is concerned, we're part of the riff raff," Tal told her. "They won't be happy when he comes back, whether it's now or in two years. I'm pretty sure they're hoping someone finishes the job on the *Oro* and saves them the trouble."

"You think they just expect us to disappear?" Lori asked, holding onto Joey tightly.

"The fact that they sent this ship out, every major system held together with duct tape and rubber bands, with only one undermanned unit to manage this many civilians? And no medic, no botanists, and not even a full colony kit in the hold." Tal looked at each of the faces around the table. "They already wrote this ship off as a total loss after the attack. They literally have nothing to lose."

"Except the thorns in their side." Sue added.

Tal nodded.

"What can we do?" asked Maisy.

"I'm not sure," Tal replied. "Keep doing what you're doing. Help people stay calm and be prepared." Tal rose from the table, maneuvering his long legs out from under the bench. "I'll let you know what's going on."

Maisy rose to stand next to him and Tal reached for her hand.

"I won't let anything happen to you, Maze." Tal stared into her eyes for a moment and then turned to the others. "To any of you. The CSS may own my contract, but as far as I'm concerned, I'm still a marine." Tal's jaw firm, he squeezed Maisy's hand one last time and turned away, moving swiftly from the room.

Maisy watched him go, her mind racing.

"Let's head back to the suite. We have a lot to think about."

14

Contingency plans

After wolfing down her breakfast, Maisy hitched her black bag onto her shoulder and slipped from the unit before anyone else was awake. Moving past the cafeteria, she entered the cargo hold where they had first disembarked onto the ship only weeks before. She hesitated for a moment in the doorway, the memories from that day rushing back.

Her eyes moved over the spot where Lori's mom had laid on the deck and she wondered what had happened to the bodies of the people who had died that day. Tal would most likely know, but she would never ask him. The wounds from that day needed to heal. For everyone.

The cargo bay was one large room, similar to an earthside warehouse. There were areas marked off with bright yellow lines and numbers on the floor for cargo, with tiedowns. About a quarter of these were stacked high with containers, each strapped to the floor. She walked toward the first cargo area and weaved her way between the containers. They were stacked nearly to the ceiling, high above her.

Referring to the manifest she'd downloaded to her tablet, Maisy searched for the correct number etched onto the floor, finally reaching the area she was looking for. According to the info they'd been able to pull off the ship's net, this stack of containers held a variety of small tools. Now, the next problem would be accessing the metal box.

She made her way back out of the maze of containers and scanned the cargo bay until her eyes picked out the shape of a loader parked against the far end of the bay, past the single remaining shuttle in its dock. Maisy noted that the shuttle ramp had been left down. She considered exploring the shuttle, but decided to leave that for later. Her number one priority for this morning was that crate.

Pulling herself into the seat of the loader, Maisy took stock of the controls. They seemed similar to the farm equipment she'd operated on Earth and fairly straightforward. She pressed the ignition and the electric engine hummed to life. When she pressed down cautiously on the accelerator, the little machine sprung forward smoothly. Within a couple of minutes she was using the crane arm on the loader to lower the container she needed to the deck.

Pulling her small pocket knife from her bag, Maisy wedged the blade into one of the seams. The container was cube shaped and nearly as tall as Maisy, so it took her a while to pry open all of the edges on one end.

Inside there were neat stacks of equipment in plastic boxes. Pulling one out, Maisy sat it on the seat of the loader. Inside was a small welding kit, a high power flashlight, a small utility knife, and various other random tools. Grabbing several boxes, Maisy pushed the container closed again and made her way back to the suite.

The corridors were empty, but inside the suite everyone was up and moving. Joanie and Leo sat at the table eating and Lori spooned a colorful mush into Joey's open mouth. Jane stood at the counter in the kitchen unit, and Sue was sitting on the bench, scrolling through the other tablet.

"Mission accomplished," Maisy announced as she walked into the unit.

Sitting her stack of boxes on the table, she slid into her chair, sharing a smile with the breakfasting children. Taking a box from the top of the stack, she sat it in front of her on the table and carefully opened the top, taking the contents out one by one and arranging them on the tabletop. Maisy looked up to see the room's other inhabitants watching her intently.

Picking up the flashlight, Maisy tested the weight in her hand. It was heavy and well-balanced. Next, she took the small torch from the welding kit. It had a safety shield attached to the front. Using the small screwdriver from the kit, Maisy pried off the guard from the front and set it aside. Lifting the altered device in her hand, Maisy squeezed the trigger. A ball of blue flame leapt out from the tip immediately, ending about a handspan away.

"Oh, wow," Joanie breathed. "What are you going to use that for?"

"We'll see," Maisy smiled. She glanced at Lori, who raised an eyebrow.

"That may come in handy," Lori said.

"In more ways than one!" Maisy nodded, putting the device away. "So far, at least, the manifest we found seems fairly accurate."

"That's good," Sue said, sliding the tablet across the table to Maisy. "Take a look at this. Container number 6733."

"What is it?" Maisy asked, hoping for more tools that could be turned into weapons. *Or actual weapons would be awesome too*, Maisy thought. But so far this was the closest they'd come to being able to arm themselves. Maisy grabbed the tablet Sue offered and scanned the list to find 6733. Below the container number was the packing list. Scanning down the items, Maisy's eyes lit up. "A medical kit?" she exclaimed.

"That might come in handy as well," Sue said.

"I'm on it," Maisy nodded, jumping up from her seat. "And I'll bring back some more of these as well."

"Can we come with you?" Joanie asked, speaking for Leo.

Maisy glanced at Sue, who nodded after a moment. Maisy turned to glance at Jane, who was leaning against the counter in the kitchen and nursing a cup of coffee. "Sure.".

Sue turned to Lori. "I can watch Joey if you want to go with them too," she offered.

Lori smiled. "That would be great. Thank you!"

Sue lifted her arms for the little boy and Lori gratefully deposited him into her lap. Joanie and Leo had already jumped up and were running for the door.

Maisy watched them all scramble for the exit and laughed. "Cabin fever?" She turned back to Sue and Jane who were both laughing as well. "We'll be back soon. Thank you!"

Sue

Sue's smile faded as she watched the door close behind Maisy. Jane sat next to her at the table, placing a fresh cup of coffee near her—but far enough away to avoid Joey's flailing arms. "It'll be okay," Jane told her.

Sue sighed, reaching for the coffee. It was synthetic and processed to hell and back, but caffeine was caffeine and she hadn't slept well in weeks.

"Will it?" Sue asked, her voice soft.

Jane slipped into her chair and took a drink from her own cup. "Well," she considered, "it probably will for the next couple of hours. Maze and Lori will make sure the kids get back here safely. As for the rest of it..." Jane trailed off. "I don't know."

Joey cooed into Sue's face, reached up to pat her cheek and then became enthralled with his own hand. Sue smiled again, watching the baby's antics.

She looked up at Jane. "Aren't you worried? Not just what will become of us, but what about the kids? They have their whole lives ahead of them and we've left civilization behind."

"Oh, I think we left civilization behind quite a while ago. I never imagined that the coalition government would pull out of the rim." Jane sat deep in thought for a moment, then continued. "If we can get away from the corporations...and build something new..."

Jane sat her cup down on the table and turned to look at Sue, her voice serious. "I had never considered the idea of being a colonist. It seems like something for men in straw hats and religious zealots. But we're here now. We're hurtling away from that mess—not just on the Citadel but on Earth as well—and while this isn't exactly the opportunity I was imagining for Leo...." Jane shrugged.

Sue was impressed by Jane's acceptance and adaptability but she wasn't sure she could match it. She just wasn't there yet. "Maybe I'll feel better about all of this when we learn a little bit about the planet." Sue grimaced. "Right now, I'm imagining an ice world inhabited by giant carnivorous spiders."

"Yeah, that would suck," Jane replied, surprising a laugh out of Sue. Joey had no idea what they were laughing about but he joined in anyway.

Maisy

Maisy added the final updates to the board and exited the app, tossing her tablet onto the bed beside her. Over the last few weeks the other refugees had been making board updates as well and it was becoming easier to communicate. They'd added a list of names and locations to help everyone get around.

She'd found a whole EDU subnetwork in the ship's network. There were modules through graduate level courses in engineering and biochemistry, to name a few. There were also thousands of gigs of literature and a huge vid library. They wouldn't be bored, at least. Assuming they survived the trip to wherever they were going.

The door to the bedroom was open and the kids were playing quietly in the living area. Rising from the bed, she went to stand in the doorway. She'd known Sue and Joanie well enough to say hello in the hallways, but she'd never even met the others before her dad's last mission. It seemed like so long ago now. So much had changed. This was her family now. And she'd figure out a way to protect them.

"It's almost 1800, so I'm going to head over to the cafeteria. You guys coming?" Maisy asked. Joanie and Leo answered enthusiastically in the affirmative. The others were slightly more subdued but everyone looked forward to the opportunity to socialize with the other passengers of the *Oro* at least once a day.

In the cafeteria, Maisy was beginning to recognize faces and associate them with names on the board. She caught up with the last group without a networked device and gave them the tablet she'd hobbled together from salvaged parts.

Returning to her group's table, Maisy smiled her thanks at the bowl of soup sitting at her spot. Lori nodded and they all began eating. Jane was making notations on a tablet between bites.

"What's our official count?" Maisy asked.

Without looking up, Jane said, "We're at one hundred and thirteen." Closing the tablet, Jane took another spoonful of her soup before looking up. "It helps that everyone sits at the same tables. It's still possible there are people afraid to leave the rooms, but I think this is probably everyone."

Maisy began to reply and was distracted by a change in the conversations around them. She looked over to see that Tal had entered the cafeteria. Catching her eye, he made his way over to their table. This time, he'd changed out of his uniform into a pair of plain black overalls. The top was unzipped to reveal a plain gray t-shirt beneath.

"No uniform?" Maisy asked.

Tal looked down, self-conscious. "No. They didn't tell us about this mission until we were already on the ship, so no one even has a change of clothes. We had to raid some of the crew's quarters."

"We did the same thing," Maisy told him. "This was not a well-planned excursion."

"No. No, it wasn't," Tal agreed. "I've been thinking about it and I'm pretty sure this was impulsive. The station manager realized they were writing off the *Oro* and someone had the brainstorm to kill two birds with one stone."

"Maybe let's not use the word *kill*," Maisy suggested. She ignored Tal's grimace and continued, "Have you been able to find out anything more about the colony?"

"Yes, but you aren't going to like it." Tal folded himself onto the bench and leaned across the table. "There is no colony. There's literally nothing there." He slid a thumbdrive across the table to Maisy. "This is everything I was able to access about the planet. There were anomalous mineral readings from the probe CT sent to the system about five years ago."

Out of his uniform, fewer people recognized Tal as a CSS agent, but there was some side-eye being directed their way. Maisy chose to ignore it, but she wasn't surprised when the cafeteria began clearing out quickly.

"What kind of readings?" Maisy asked. She froze for a moment and whipped her head toward Tal. "Radiation?" she asked, holding her breath.

"No!" Tal said quickly, waving a hand. "Not quite that bad. They didn't actually even land a probe on the surface. They did a high level atmo run and all levels were well within livable range. The analysis is on that drive."

"Is that all of the bad news?" Maisy asked, pushing her empty soup bowl away. She put her elbows on the table, bracing herself mentally.

"Well, the surface of the planet is mostly water—which is why they didn't try to land the probe. Looks like there's only one fairly small continent."

"Okay..." Maisy waited for the other shoe to drop. "And..."

"And there appears to be quite a bit of indigenous life."

"So like...water planet filled with monsters is what you're saying?"

"Pretty much, yeah." Tal sighed, leaning his elbow on the table and resting his head on his hand.

"Great. Thanks." Maisy pocketed the thumbdrive and met Tal's resigned gaze. "Anything else I should know?"

Tal hesitated.

Maisy sighed aggressively. "There's no point in pussyfooting around, Tal." Maisy gestured to the women around the table and then swept her arm to include the almost empty room. "We all know how bad things are for us down here. What's the situation on the bridge?"

"It's not good," Tal admitted.

His wrist unit buzzed and Tal glanced at the screen. "Crap, I have to go." Unfolding himself from the table, he looked down at Maisy, his brow furrowed. "I'll try to come back down tomorrow."

"Okay." As he turned away, Maisy grabbed his hand. "Be careful, Tal. I'll see you tomorrow."

Tal's expression cleared and he squeezed Maisy's hand before releasing her and walking quickly from the room. Maisy stared after him for a moment, lost in thought.

"He cares about you," Sue said.

Startled, Maisy remembered the others and turned back to the table to see everyone watching her intently.

"Oh, please," she scoffed, ignoring the sudden warmth in her face. "He hero-worshipped my dad. We're just lucky he's on board."

Sue smiled. "While I'm sure both of those things are true, what I said is as well. That boy is trying to do the right thing, but his number one priority is definitely you."

"Sue," Maisy said very firmly, "I have absolutely zero ability to deal with Tal or anyone else's romantic intentions at the moment." When Sue continued to smile in the face of Maisy's rebuke, she turned to Lori for help.

"Back me up here?" But the traitorous redhead just laughed and shook her head.

"I think he's cute," Lori confessed as she rose from the table, Joey on her hip. "Sorry!" she said unrepentantly as she gathered the dirty dishes from the table and walked them over to the recycler.

Maisy rolled her eyes hard and stood as well, ready to head back to the room.

15

Tal's afternoon

Tal

Tal stepped off the elevator and made his way quickly toward the bridge. As he walked through the doorway, Joe caught his eye and shook his head minutely, exhaustion hanging from his face.

Great, thought Tal, *Tratt is in a mood again*.

It had begun to occur to him that this wasn't actually a mood, but rather the old man's personality. This was not a happy conclusion to come to.

Moving quietly into position at his station, Tal checked across the board. There were still a considerable number of red lights, but he didn't expect that to change. There were compartments open to space and the team had accepted that there was little they could do to get the ship back to all greens. Indeed, the insurance company had reached the same conclusion, which was why the *Oro* had been labeled a write off.

The fact that this ship was still space worthy was dumb luck. Really, the fact that it hadn't exploded out by the asteroid field was extraordinarily lucky in and of itself. If only the *Sky* had been so lucky. Tal pushed those thoughts away firmly and forced himself to focus on the task at hand.

"Thank you for joining us, Mr. Buchanan." The captain's voice cut across the unnatural silence of the bridge.

Rosa, sitting at the weapon's station, didn't raise her eyes from her console, but a smirk twisted her lips. She and the pilot, Bill, were the only two members of Tratt's original crew and their first loyalty was to the captain. Bill was quiet but Rosa seemed to enjoy the drama of Tratt's violent mood swings and was more interested in basking in the chaos of their situation than worrying about the ship's safety.

Like Tal and Joe, the sixth member of their team had been added to Unit 7 right before this mission. Berta was technically Tratt's first officer, but Tal knew Tratt didn't trust her and she hadn't been given any of the traditional responsibilities of a first officer.

"I was checking on our passengers, sir," Tal said carefully.

"Our *prisoners*," Tratt corrected.

"The colonists, sir." Tal said firmly and Tratt barked out a derisive laugh.

"That fantasy is for them, not you, boy," Tratt scoffed. "You know as well as I do that there's no colony and this is a one way trip."

Tal frowned at Tratt's words. Since they'd come aboard the ship, the captain's language in regard to the passengers had continued to escalate. Tratt was dehumanizing them and demonizing them all toward one goal.

"Our orders are to drop these people off on 761 and return to the station. I haven't received any information to countermand those orders, sir." Tal was pushing the line with Tratt, but he could see the captain convincing himself that those orders didn't matter.

Tal knew that Tratt may very well be right. There was a very good chance that the station management was counting on Tratt's bad faith. It would certainly tidy things up neatly from their perspective. Not to mention saving two years of the crew's salaries. But no matter how much Tal might not want to be out here, past the edge of the rim, he wasn't willing to murder over one hundred people to avoid it. Even if one of those people wasn't Maisy Renner.

Tal acknowledged that it wasn't just his loyalty to Jackson Renner that made him determined to protect Maisy. He'd known she was smart and capable when they'd first met, but since the destruction of the *Sky,* he'd seen her compassion and selflessness too. He'd tried to find her right after his return to the Citadel but there'd been no answer at the door to Jackson's unit and he'd hit a dead end.

Tal's reassignment to station security had sidelined everything else. He'd known that legally, all of the s-marines on the station had been converted to CSS contracts but it hadn't actually affected them on the *Sky*. Then the *Sky* and most of her crew were gone. After floating in space for two days waiting for rescue, Tal had been shellshocked when he and Joe had finally made it back to the station. His only thought had been to find Maisy, to tell her what had happened to Jackson.

Tal had *needed* to tell Maisy what had happened.

And instead he'd found himself walking around the station in a black helmet, carrying a shockstick. He'd been assigned to the team relocating the residents of the lowest decks of the station. There were three groups.

The first, Tal realized now, was the luckiest. They were joining the other Cits being moved off of the station. They weren't all happy to go, but Tal and the other officers were able to escort them to the transport with minimal fuss. Families from all over the station were being reassigned to other facilities. The word from Corporate was that the Citadel facility was being "streamlined"—whatever that meant—and optimized to increase processing capacity.

It had felt like an evacuation.

The second group were the ones being relocated to the higher decks of the station. They too were generally happy with their circumstances. The temperatures had already increased as the processing facility output went up and people had started to notice. The lowest levels were already uncomfortable.

The biggest mistake of the operation was not giving residents time to move their belongings. Everything happened so quickly that people weren't able to pack. It raised huge red flags with residents who would otherwise have been happy to move up the physical representation of the corporate hierarchy.

Then there was the third group. The people that Citatech didn't find valuable enough to move or who they wanted to get rid of for one reason or another. Some of the QC and safety monitors were moved to other facilities, but most were considered redundant. Anyone associated with the SIWU, the union for space installation workers, was considered redundant. Anyone who complained was considered a troublemaker. And they were all designated as "colonists".

It had been a shock to see Maisy among them. He'd seen the red haired girl with the baby and mentioned them to his commander, but the man hadn't cared. Tal was horrified that they were sending an infant to a remote colony. Especially with a young girl who didn't even look old enough to be the baby's mother. Nothing about the operation was well-thought out. Tal had bought food for the baby with his own credits—and he'd been devastated when Maisy had opened the door.

Tal had still been reeling from that discovery when he'd found out that the so-called "colony ship" was actually the wreck of the *Oro Zapato*.

He'd gone to Tindell Burt, the head of station security. The man had laughed in his face. By the time Tal returned to the lower decks, he'd been reassigned to Unit 7. He knew it was a punishment, but Tal was happy to be going. Then he'd reported to Tratt and found that Joe was also aboard the *Oro*.

Tal's parents had been older when he'd been born via a surrogate. They'd decided late in life they wanted a child to dote on, but the reality of an infant in the golden years of their life had not met their expectations.

He'd been raised by a series of poorly paid au pairs until he was old enough to be self-sufficient. His family wasn't close and it hadn't been a huge blow when both of his parents had passed while he was in college, but it had left him adrift. Enlisting had fulfilled his need to be a part of a real family.

As a member of the crew of the *Sky*, Tal had felt like he belonged for the first time in his life. Having had that ripped away, he was more than happy to be racing away from civilization on the shot-out haul of a derelict freighter, knowing that Joe and Maisy, the last two connections to that family, were on board.

Tal was jolted from his thoughts by a new red light on his board. The output on one of the remaining engines had dropped out of acceptable parameters. Given their already depleted capabilities, this could become a huge problem quickly.

"Captain, we have an issue with engine number three." Tal tabbed through the readouts, comparing the historical values. "It looks like a coolant issue. There's a redundant system but it isn't engaging automatically." Tal looked up to see that Tratt had called the data onto his own screen and was scrolling through the numbers.

"Get down there and check it out," he said abruptly, closing the window.

"Yes, sir," Tal replied.

Happy for an excuse to get off the bridge, Tal took the elevator down to the engineering level and jogged past the other units to number three. Inside the door, he opened the supply closet to grab a tool kit and belted it around his waist.

The engine room was built around a large reactor coil protruding into the center of the room. The coolant tubes ran along both sides of the coil. Upon visual inspection everything seemed intact but when he scanned the coolant tubes with the detector in his toolkit, he identified two separate microscopic leaks. He applied sealant and cured the patches with a UV light, retesting to confirm that the leaks had been fixed.

Replacing the tools back into the kit, Tal pulled up the coolant monitor on the panel built into the wall beside the door. The light was still red and a quick check revealed that the coolant level had dropped too low to maintain the system and the temperature in the main coil was still rising.

Tal rifled through the storage areas in the room but there were no canisters of coolant. Exiting engine room three, he jogged to the next unit. Engine two had been taken offline in the pirate attack. The ship had received a cursory overhaul while docked at the station, but it seemed to have been more of a safety inspection than any actual repairs. Tapping on the panel beside the door, the display showed that engine two was offline but there were no atmosphere warnings.

Opening the door cautiously, Tal glanced around the room. Everything appeared intact and there were no obvious issues. All of the panels were dark and the engine had been completely shut down. Tal opened the supply cabinet near the door and looked through the contents. Again, there was no coolant. It was standard practice to have extra coolant near each engine and Tal wondered if it had been used during the initial attack...or if it had been scavenged from the ship while it was in dock.

This could be a problem, he thought as he rummaged through the storage area under the main panel.

Flying back out into the hall, he ran down to the next engine room. This engine was up and running, all lights green across the board. But no coolant in either of the supply compartments.

Tal ran back out into the hall and jogged back the way he'd come, past the other two engine compartments. The blast doors were closed between engines three and four and Tal knew from the damage reports that engine four had been completely destroyed and the compartment was open to space. He'd have to go down three levels to get past the breach and around to the other engines.

"Report, Mr. Buchanan!" Tratt's voice barked out of Tal's wrist unit, making him jump.

"Crap," he muttered as he fumbled for the control. "The leak is sealed, Captain," Tal reported, "but the engine is low on coolant and I'm not having any luck finding any in supplies. I've checked the first three compartments. There's a breach down here and it's going to take me a while to get around it. I'm going to have to shut down the engine until we can replace the coolant." Tal grimaced, bracing himself for Tratt's response.

The captain did not disappoint. "The hell you say, boy! Don't touch that engine. I'm sending Rosa down to help you do your job." Tal nodded to himself, rolling his eyes to the ceiling.

"Yes, sir," he responded, closing the channel. *Great. That will definitely make things better.*

Walking back into the compartment for engine three, Tal checked the status. There were now three red lights and the temperature was getting higher. If he didn't shut down the engine soon, the system would do it automatically.

Opening the channel with the bridge, he spoke into his wrist unit, "Captain, if you want me to wait in engine three for Rosa, can you send Joe to engine five to check for coolant reserves?"

There was no response for several moments, then Joe responded, "I'm on it, Tal."

Knowing that base was covered, Tal rubbed a hand over his jaw, considering their options. He understood Tratt's reaction. Losing one of the remaining engines would increase their travel time. If there was no coolant on board, they'd need to either make it from whatever they could scrounge up—lubricant?—or they'd have to recover it from one of the damaged engines.

From what Tal knew of the reactor coil type engines like those of the *Oro*, recovering coolant from the system was theoretically possible...but it wouldn't be easy. It would definitely take longer than they had before engine three overheated.

Tall accessed the engine schematic on the panel above the coil. According to the display, three of the *Oro*'s engines were offline. Engine two looked like it was intact, and there was no sign of what the issue there had been. There was only mild damage on the exterior. Number four was just gone. Six had been severely damaged as well, so it made sense that five had issues. The other two engines on the port side of the ship were all in the green and carrying the bulk of the load.

"Step away from the engine!" demanded a shrill voice from the doorway. Rosa charged into the compartment, arms akimbo.

"What is your issue?" Tal asked, trying to keep his cool.

"You're the one with an issue, Buchanan," Rosa replied snidely. Under other circumstances, Tal might have thought Rosa was beautiful. But her loyalty to Tratt seemed to twist something inside of her. Tal didn't think their relationship was improper by s-marine—or CSS—standards, but it definitely wasn't healthy. Rosa fed off of Tratt's irrational rage, constantly fanning the flames higher.

"Did you tell the old man that I was trying to sabotage the ship?" Tal asked incredulously. When Rosa just smirked in response, Tal shook his head. "Why? What's the point?"

Tal didn't expect an answer. Stepping out of the engine compartment, he began jogging toward the nearest access ladder at the end of the hallway. Tapping his wrist unit Tal opened a channel to the bridge. "Rosa has relieved me in the engine compartment. I'm going to help Joe look for more coolant." Tal cut the channel quickly as he stepped into the access shaft.

Within minutes, Tal was running down the hallway on the port side of the ship, having crossed three decks below the burned out hull of engine four. He spotted Joe leaving one of the compartments and called out.

Joe turned toward the sound of Tal's voice, his face tight with worry. "Tal! I've got bad news and worse news."

"No coolant?" Tal guessed.

"That's the bad news," Joe confirmed. "The worse news is that it looks like engine five is on its last leg. Berta confirmed it's showing green on the bridge but the panel in the compartment is flashing red on coolant as well."

"Oh, hell."

"Exactly." Joe shook his head. "This is precisely why ships this size don't go out with a skeleton crew. This ship needs twice as many people to run it safely—minimum!"

Tal knew Joe was right, but there was nothing he could do about it. Or that anyone could do about it at this point.

"So we're about to lose two engines? The old man is going to lose it," Tal predicted.

"The minute you left the bridge he started foaming. You need to watch your back." Joe turned his back to the wall and slid down to sit on the floor of the corridor. "This is bad, man. I'm not sure this ship can make it to 761, much less make it back to the Citadel. CT just gave us a one way ticket to the recycler."

Tal laughed at Joe, running his hands through his hair. "So we've been downgraded from organ donors to floating space trash. Good to know."

"Laugh all you want, kid, but there is no exit strategy for Unit 7. This is a one way trip, man," Joe moaned as he dropped his head to his hands.

"What are you talking about? Get up, Joe, and help me find some coolant before this block of swiss cheese slows to a crawl."

"I've checked all of the storage compartments on this side. There's nothing." Joe lifted his head to look at Tal intently. "And what are the chances we'll need more in the next freakin' two years it takes to get back to the station, huh?"

"Yes, this is a problem," Tal said calmly. "Let's not give up just yet, though, okay? I'm going to go through and check this side again. Can you double check the first three, in case I missed something?" Tal reached down a hand to his friend.

Joe sat on the floor, weighing his options and considering Tal's hand, and finally let loose a huge sigh and accepted the assistance to heave himself to his feet.

"You realize this is entirely pointless, right?" Joe asked, dusting himself off. "We're not even a month into a two year long mission and we've already run into major mechanical issues. This ship will never make it all the way there and back."

"We'll make it," Tal said firmly.

"And even if we did," Joe continued, ignoring him, "don't think we'd be greeted with open arms upon our return. I'm telling you, Unit 7 was thrown out with the trash. This whole mission is the Corporation killing two birds with one stone."

Tal didn't reply, not wanting to encourage Joe's paranoid rant, but his confusion must have shown on his face. "Don't you get it, man? Tratt's unit got creamed by the same pirates who took out the *Sky*. We're an embarrassment. And those Cits are dead weight. This whole mission is just a way for Corporate to get rid of both of us."

Tal didn't want to admit that Joe might be right. And really, it didn't change the situation they were in right now.

"Our number one priority needs to be those engines, Joe," Tal said gently. "Let's put this fire out and then we can work on the next problem, okay?"

Joe shook his head, his shoulders sagging. "Yeah, man. I'll check out the other compartments and meet you back on the bridge. The fireworks should at least be entertaining." Joe slapped Tal on the upper arm as he turned away and started back down the hallway toward the access ladder.

Tal stood, watching him go for a moment before starting to enter the engine compartment. He paused, remembering that Rosa might still be in engine three. Glancing toward the access shaft, Tal saw that Joe had already disappeared from sight.

I probably should have warned him, he thought.

16

Mutiny on the Golden Shoe

Tal

An hour later, Tal took a deep breath before walking back onto the bridge. The minute he entered the room, every face turned his way. Engine three had taken itself offline about thirty minutes ago, as Tal had predicted. Joe was standing at his station and he gave Tal a small shake of his head as they made eye contact.

"Report," the captain barked.

Wondering what Joe was trying to communicate, Tal answered cautiously, "We've checked all engine compartments several times and there's no replacement coolant on board. I heard the warning for engine three going offline. I think we can cannibalize parts from engine two. It will take a while but I think we can get three back up and running within a couple of days at most."

"Unacceptable," Tratt snapped.

"Engine five may hold until we can pull what we need out of number two, but it would be prudent to shut it down now just in case."

"*Five?*" the captain screeched. "What's wrong with engine five?"

As Tratt started ranting, Tal closed his eyes for a moment, understanding the significance of Joe's look. He hadn't told Tratt anything. *Thanks, Joe.*

Taking a deep breath, Tal began calmly, "Engine number four was completely destroyed. The blast rocked the coils on both sides and caused microleaks in three and five. The leaks are now repaired, but the engines have lost too much coolant to maintain their temperatures in the safe range. In addition, the coils in number five are badly out of alignment. Realigning them isn't difficult but it will take a day or so."

Tal watched in concern as Tratt's face turned red, then purple. He glanced around the room, looking to his crewmates for help. Rosa and Joe were watching the interaction like a tennis match. Joe looked increasingly anxious and Rosa's face glowed with barely concealed glee. The pilot, Bill, was carefully keeping his eyes on his console and not looking at anyone. Berta was watching Tratt with concern, and looked ready to intervene.

Tal caught Berta's gaze, hoping the captain's second would step in to diffuse the situation. She opened her mouth to speak, then her eyes went wide as they slid past Tal's shoulder. He turned to follow her gaze. Maisy was framed in the doorway to the bridge once again. *Crap*, Tal thought with a sense of deja vu.

"What's going on?" Maisy asked urgently. "We heard the emergency shutdown warning and the passengers are all worried and need to know what's going on." Maisy stood firmly in the doorway, her mass of curly hair pulled back, accentuating her long neck. She flicked her eyes over Tal in acknowledgement but moved her gaze back to Tratt as the captain leaped up from his chair.

"Passengers? Passengers!" the old man screamed, spittal flying. "Rats! Cockroaches!" he screeched, flying across the bridge toward Maisy, who stumbled back out into the corridor.

Tal inserted himself between Tratt and the doorway, block-ing Maisy from the Captain's view. Berta appeared at Tal's side, speaking quickly and quietly to the captain.

Tratt didn't slow down.

Like a bull who'd seen red, he straight-armed Berta, nearly knocking her off her feet, and plowed his shoulder into Tal's. Tal had a couple of inches on the captain, but the older man was broader and it felt like hitting a wall.

Tal shook off the blow and followed the captain, Berta right behind him. Past Tratt, Maisy had ducked into the elevator, her face pale. Tal reached out, ready to grab Tratt. His hand hovered over the captain's shoulder as the elevator doors finally slid shut.

Maisy

Maisy slipped her hand into the pocket of her cargo pants, palming the small pocket knife nestled within as the elevator doors slid shut between her and Tratt. Sagging back against the rear wall of the elevator, Maisy's heart pounded as the elevator descended, her entire body vibrating. She took sev-eral deep, slow breaths and tried to consciously release the adrenaline from her system.

"Well, that was fun," Maisy muttered to herself as she slipped out of the elevator. She headed toward the cafeteria, not surprised to see even more people had gathered there since her foray to the bridge. As she walked through the door, the low buzz of conversation got louder, then faded.

Maisy walked to where her group was gathered around their usual table. Rather than sitting on the bench, Maisy braced her foot on it and sat on the tabletop, feet firmly on the scat. She leaned forward and rested her elbows on her knees. Around the room, there were men and women seated at tables and gathered in small groups. They all looked at her expectantly.

Turning to Lori, Maisy said softly, "Take the kids and bring back the equipment boxes. We're going to need them." Lori nodded, handing Joey to Sue, and gestured for Joanie and Leo to follow her. Maisy watched them disappear through the cafeteria doors before she started talking.

"We have a problem," Maisy began. As if her words lifted a magic spell, the room filled with conversation again.

"Are the engines offline?"

"Can they be fixed?"

"What happened? Why isn't the captain talking to us?"

The questions came from multiple directions, voices raised in concern and full of urgency. Maisy held up her hands and the passengers quieted again.

"I have a plan."

Tal

Tal's stomach was tied in knots and sweat ran down his forehead. He walked behind Tratt, even his long legs struggling to keep up with the older man's determined stride. Behind them, the other members of Unit 7 were breaking into a trot, their faces expressing varying levels of concern.

"Sir, we can't abandon our mission," Tal insisted for the tenth time.

"There is no mission, boy," Tratt responded shortly. "I'm the captain and I'm pulling the plug. We're aborting this mission."

His voice was calm and firm. Tratt's earlier fury had given way to a cold determination.

"You can't just leave these people out here to die!" Tal insisted.

"These people are already dead, Buchanan. They're just too stupid to realize it," Tratt responded dispassionately.

"They'll court-martial you!" Tal cried desperately.

At that pronouncement, Tratt stopped abruptly and spun to face Tal, who almost ran into him.

"Who will court martial me, boy? When will you finally get it through your head that we're not marines anymore?" Tratt stabbed a finger at Tal's chest, hard enough to bruise under Tal's gray t-shirt. "Citatech isn't going to court martial me. They'll give me a fucking bonus for bringing that shuttle back." Tratt turned away from Tal and continued down the corridor. "It's the only thing on this damn ship that has any value."

"Sir," Tal tried again, "if you take the shuttle, then the colonists will have no way to get to the surface when they arrive at 761."

Tratt laughed humorlessly. "These people aren't going to make it to that planet, Buchanan, and you know it. Engine five will shut down at any moment and speed will be reduced by another twenty percent. There's no way this ship will hold together long enough to get them there." Tratt stopped again, swinging around to face Tal and the rest of his crew behind him.

"Don't be naive, Buchanan," Tratt said firmly. "These people were never meant to set foot on that planet."

Tal stared at the captain, at a loss for words.

"The whole point of this mission was to get them off the station. Mission accomplished." Tratt's smile sent chills down Tal's spine.

Joe stepped up to Tal's side. "He has a point, man, I'm sorry."

Tal turned to face Joe, agog. "Are you kidding me? You're going to go along with this crazy logic?"

"It's not crazy," Joe insisted. "It's actually the only thing that makes sense. You know as well as I do that these people are not *colonists*." Joe sneered at the word. "They're on this ship because they were causing problems on the station and Corporate wanted them gone." Joe gestured around the corridor. "And this is certainly no colony ship. This bucket has more holes than a block of swiss cheese. The ship was a write-off and Corporate decided to kill two birds with one stone."

Tal winced at the word *kill.* He had definitely been spending too much time with Maisy. "We can't just leave these people out here to die. What about the children? The baby?"

The captain laughed again. "I told you, boy. They're already dead. The only question left to answer is whether or not you're going to stay here and die with them." Having delivered that statement, the captain turned away from Tal dismissively and stepped into the elevator, Rosa right behind him. The other four members of the team hesitated and ducked into the elevator after him. Tal slipped in as the doors began to slide shut.

"Sir, if you take the shuttle, then even if the *Oro* makes it to 761, they'll have no way to get down to the surface. This ship isn't built to land dirtside—and they won't even have a pilot!" Tal was becoming increasingly desperate to break through to Tratt. The captain's anger seemed to have completely disappeared and in its place was a cold determination to abandon the ship—and its passengers.

Tratt turned to Bill, waving his hand carelessly. "Bill, you're welcome to stay here with the boy and the riffraff and try to land this ship on the surface of 761. Rosa and I are both more than capable of piloting the shuttle back to the Citadel." The elevator doors opened and Tratt walked out with a swing to his step. "I'll pass my condolences on to your next of kin," Tratt called over his shoulder. At his side, Rosa looked back at Tal with a smirk.

Tal met Bill's eyes. They were full of the resignation as the older man turned to follow the captain. Joe hurried out after Bill but Berta hesitated. Tal looked at her searchingly.

"Are you going to go along with this?" he asked. They hadn't worked together long, but Tal had been impressed with Berta's handling of Tratt's mood swings and her ability to keep the crew going under these unusual circumstances. He knew that she hadn't been a member of Tratt's previous crew but he didn't know what had happened to her original unit. Since they'd boarded the *Oro,* she'd been quiet, but competent.

Berta broke eye contact with Tal and walked out of the elevator without acknowledging his question.

Tal stood frozen for a moment, overwhelmed by the absurdity of the situation. The elevator doors started closing again, jolting him into movement. Lurching from the car, Tal raced down the hallway after the rest of his unit, his mind ticking over his options.

He wished he had a way to contact Maisy at that moment, but he knew there was nothing a teenage girl could do to make his decision any easier. The captain wasn't wrong. The chances of them reaching 761 on this ship were slim...but Tal knew if the captain carried out his plan, those chances dropped to zero. That was an outcome Tal couldn't live with.

Rounding the corner to the cargo bay, Tal nearly ran into Berta's back. The rest of the unit stood frozen in the corridor, staring at the entrance to the cargo bay. The doors were sealed shut, an uneven, bulging line of welding all along the seam. One of Maisy's friends slipped past Tal and he watched her duck into the elevator, his brain putting two and two together.

"What the hell...?" Tratt said, his voice trailing off as his calm faded and his face grew red. The rage inside him built and spilled over as he too grasped the situation.

"Rats!" he screamed. "Cockroaches! Come out here and face me!" Tratt pulled the shockstick from his belt and whipped around, brandishing it wildly.

From the other end of the hall, the sound of approaching footsteps sounded. Tratt spun to face the noise, struck
speechless for a moment as dozens of men and women approached, each brandishing large flashlights like clubs.

At the front of the crowd stood Maisy Renner.

17

Bon voyage

Maisy

Maisy watched the elevator seal shut, whisking Jane up to the bridge. Step two of their plan was underway. They'd already sealed the cargo bay to prevent the captain from stealing the shuttle, now Jane was heading to the bridge to lock herself in and try to gain access to the final command modules they couldn't hack into remotely. The third part of the plan was up to her. They had an offer for Captain Tratt, and his response would determine how the next few minutes played out.

"Good evening, Captain. You weren't thinking of leaving us, were you?" Maisy asked calmly, stepping forward. The older man was still standing with his shockstick in his hand, his face red.

"You!" the captain spat. "Renner's brat. What have you done?"

"I've prevented you from a dereliction of duty, Captain," Maisy replied baldly.

Tratt sputtered for a moment, his color still high. "Open these doors, you little cockroach!" he finally got out.

"No." Maisy said firmly. "Taking the shuttle is no longer an option for you." Maisy let Tratt sputter and flail for a moment, her expression impassive in the face of his rage. "You have two options left to you, Captain."

"You don't tell me what my options are, girl! I'm in charge here!" Tratt raised the hand with the shockstick again, although Maisy wasn't sure he even remembered he was holding it.

Maisy continued as if Tratt hadn't spoken. "You may walk yourself and your crew down to the cryochamber and sleep for the rest of this trip. We'll wake you up when it's time to return the *Oro* to the Citadel. Or you may take one of the emergency pods and take your chances on being picked up now while we're still close to the shipping lanes. The choice is yours, sir."

Maisy glanced past Tratt to the other members of Unit 7. "And, of course, each of your crewmates." She deliberately avoided looking at Tal. He would make his own decision.

Tratt was still sputtering, his face an alarming shade of purple. He looked at the cargo bay doors, his rage palpable, and back at Maisy, with murder in his eyes.

Maisy wasn't surprised when he sprang forward in her direction, shockstick raised over his head. She adjusted the grip on her heavy duty flashlight, feeling the well-balanced tool warm in her fist. As Tratt approached, his arm raised to swing down at her, Maisy swung the flashlight up and across her body to connect with the bottom of his jaw and placed her boot in his stomach, launching him backward.

Tratt's head snapped back and his feet flew up as his body traveled across the deck, skidding to a stop against the wall on the other side of the corridor in a tangle of limbs.

Everyone in the hallway outside of the cargo bay stood frozen for a moment, staring at the captain in shock and horror. He didn't move.

"Well," Maisy said, "that was easier—"

An ear-splitting screech sounded a second before a body crashed into her from the side, sending them both sailing across the deck. Maisy found herself lying on her back, a flailing demon on top of her raining down blows. The woman was about her size but built on more solid lines and pain exploded through Maisy's ribcage as the woman pounded into her, screaming into her face.

"You're nothing but trash!" the woman screeched, her breath hot as Maisy tried to twist away. A solid blow hit her stomach and Maisy reared up with a cry. She grabbed a handful of the woman's dark hair, twisting and pulling as she dragged her attacker down. The woman was still screaming insults as Maisy threw her own weight to the right, hand still firmly in her hair.

Maisy realized she'd lost her flashlight during the fall, and as she rolled over the other woman, she sat up and scanned the ground around them. Spotting the dull black cylinder by the woman's head, Maisy reached forward and grabbed it, her hand closing over it as the other woman's fist connected with the side of her head.

"Cockroach! Rat!" She continued to scream as Maisy clenched her thighs to keep from being thrown off. Her eyes watered and her face burned but she didn't go over.

Rearing up over the woman, Maisy raised the flashlight over her head. The other woman anchored her fist into Maisy's shirt, trying to pull her down, and Maisy swung the flashlight down with all of her strength.

"We—," the flashlight connected with the woman's temple and she reared up. Maisy whipped the flashlight back up and slammed it into her head again, "—are—" Stunned, her attacker released her hold on Maisy's shirt and her upper body flopped back down on the floor. "—human!"

Maisy's body sagged as she panted, the woman below her finally quiet, blood trickling from a cut on her forehead. Maisy's face throbbed, pain stabbing through her ribcage with every breath, but she knew they weren't done yet. She swung her leg awkwardly off her unconscious attacker, catching herself on the floor. She paused beside the woman's prone figure, kneeling on the floor of the corridor, bracing herself to try to rise to her feet, when suddenly a hand grabbed her elbow, pulling her up.

Maisy looked up to see Tal at her side, his face drawn and worried.

"Are you okay?" Tal asked.

Maisy nodded, still catching her breath. "I'm better than she is," Maisy gasped, gesturing at the woman on the floor.

Sue and another passenger stepped up from the crowd, lengths of plastic cord in their hands. Sue crouched by the woman and rolled her body over face down with slightly more force than necessary. Maneuvering her arms behind her, Sue tied the woman's hands together at the small of her back. The other passenger did the same for the captain, who was beginning to show signs of consciousness.

Maisy looked down at the woman at her feet.

"She's breathing, right?" Maisy was pleased that her breathing was back to normal, although her heart was still pounding.

"Yup," Sue answered, "she's fine. Although she'll have a hell of a headache when she wakes up."

"Good." Maisy said shortly. *That will make two of us.*

Tal was still holding onto her elbow and Maisy stepped back from him, turning to take in the remaining members of Unit 7.

"Are we done?" Maisy asked aggressively, blood-splattered flashlight still clutched in her fist.

"We're done," Joe responded quickly, hands up.

Maisy turned toward the two older members of the unit, a man and a woman. "And you?"

The man just held up his hands and stepped back. The woman shook her head. "I'm sorry it came to this. I know Tratt was wrong," she said in a firm voice.

Finally, Maisy turned to Tal. "What about you?" she asked quietly, her aggression draining away.

"I'm so sorry, Maze," Tal swept Maisy into his arms. She fought against the urge to sag against him. She just needed to hold it all together a little longer, then she could go back to the room and have a good cry. But not yet.

Maisy placed a gentle but firm hand against Tal's chest and stepped back. She looked again at the members of Unit 7.

"You all need to make a decision. Emergency pods or cryochambers." She finally looked up into Tal's face. "Or you can stay with the *Oro* and become colonists. We're not sure what we'll find on 761, but you're welcome to join us and find out."

Tal stared down at Maisy, saying nothing. She glanced at the others and saw they were all lost in thought, gears turning.

"I'll take my chances in a pod," Joe said. Tal's head whipped around and he stared at his friend in shock.

"Are you serious?" he asked.

"As a heart attack, man. I'm not cut out for this colony stuff, and I don't want to wake up to find myself a year further from Earth." Joe shook his head. "I'll take my chances right here, right now. We're close enough to the main shipping lanes at this point that we should get picked up pretty quickly."

A prickle of hurt tightened her chest at the thought that her father's friend was so eager to abandon them, but she nodded, respecting his decision.

"I'll go with you," the older man said quietly. He walked up to Maisy, hand extended. "I'm Bill. I'm a pilot and you'll need my help."

Maisy shook his hand, nodding solemnly. "I'm Maisy. Thank you, Bill. You don't want to try to get back to the Citadel. Or Earth...?"

"There isn't really anything back there for me. Being a marine was all I had and that's gone now, too. I never had any desire to work for the corporation." Bill shrugged, his lips twisting in a small smile. "Besides, being a colonist might be fun."

Maisy laughed in surprise, some of her tension easing. Having a pilot on board definitely increased their chances of survival. She turned to the older woman, meeting her eyes expectantly.

"I guess I'm in the same boat as Bill." She glanced at Bill with a small smile. "I'm in too." She offered her hand to Maisy, who accepted it gratefully. "I'm Berta."

"Thank you," Maisy said sincerely. Taking a deep breath, Maisy braced herself and finally turned to Tal.

"What about you?" she asked quietly.

Tal stared down at her. He'd been silent since Joe's pronouncement and Maisy had no idea what he was thinking.

"I'm sticking around, Maze. Just try to get rid of me."

Something in her chest released. Tal was her last connection with her father. And Jackson had been her last connection to her mother. She knew her emotional connection to him was less about Tal as a person but more of a reflection of how much she'd lost over the past few months. This motley group of friends, neighbors, and adhoc roommates were the closest thing she had to family these days, so she was relieved not to be losing any more of them.

With that thought, Maisy turned to Joe, who was watching the others dispassionately. She wanted to ask him if he was sure, try to talk him out of leaving, but she didn't.

"Cockroaches!"

At the hoarse scream, Maisy looked over to see that the captain had fully recovered. Waking to find himself trussed like a Thanksgiving turkey had not improved the man's demeanor at all. "Rats!" he cried. "Release me this instant!" Tratt thrashed on the floor, his hands and ankles bound tightly, while a passenger silently stood watch over him, arms crossed, staring at the former captain judgmentally.

On the other side of the corridor, the young woman who had attacked Maisy had also gained consciousness, but she was lying quietly, pinned to the floor by Sue's death stare.

Maisy touched her ribs gingerly, wondering if anything was broken. Tal reached out and touched her cheekbone.

"Rosa really got you," he said gently. "You're going to have some spectacular bruises tomorrow."

"I'm more worried about my ribs." Maisy prodded herself gingerly. "I think I'm okay. Honestly, for a couple of marines they went down surprisingly easy." Maisy smirked as Tratt escalated his thrashing and name-calling. The other woman, Rosa, continued to fume silently. Tal just shook his head, hiding a small smile.

"Let's get these three on their way." Two of the passengers hefted Tratt to his feet and Sue and Maisy grabbed Rosa between them and lifted her up. As soon as the woman was on her feet, she tried to lunge toward Maisy, but Sue had her securely by the elbow and pulled her firmly back.

"You'll never get away with this," Rosa hissed as she stumbled her way toward the emergency pods. "This is *mutiny* and you'll be *executed!*"

Maisy burst into laughter. "Well, first of all, none of us are marines—including you. Secondly, all we did was prevent your cowardly captain from abandoning ship. And third..." Maisy paused as they reached the door of the pod room. "No one cares. The Coalition Government doesn't care. The Citadel doesn't care. *No one* is going to follow us past the edge of the rim to avenge you or your captain."

The two men restraining Tratt wrestled the captain into one of the four man emergency pods docked into the hull of the ship. They forced his head down as they maneuvered him through the hatch and pushed him into a seat, anchoring him into the five point harness. Mission accomplished, they exited the pod, nodding to Sue and Maisy as they passed on their way out of the room.

"Your turn." Maisy pushed and pulled Rosa toward the pod. Once they had the woman strapped in, Maisy followed Sue from the pod. The other members of Unit 7 stood in the room, eyes focused on the hatch.

Maisy turned to Joe, giving him a long considering look. He didn't meet her eyes, his gaze ricocheting off the hatch, the floor, anywhere else.

"Good luck, Joe," Maisy said quietly.

Joe took a deep breath and seemed to settle. He finally looked at Maisy. If he'd been afraid he'd see censure in her eyes, it wasn't there.

"You, too, Maze." Joe smiled, sadly. "Your dad was a good man. I'm sorry." Maisy nodded but Joe was already ducking through the hatch into the emergency pod. He strapped himself into one of the remaining seats, ignoring his two fuming crewmates.

"Good luck, Joe," Berta called. Bill waved but remained silent.

Tal lifted a hand to Joe, then reached over and closed the hatch, pushing the door until it clicked. He glanced at Maisy, who gave him a nod, and Tal hit the pod release. The vibration reverberated through the room as the pod disengaged from the hull of the *Oro* and moved quickly away from the ship.

Their small group walked in silence back toward the cafeteria. As they approached the last turn, it became obvious that a small herd of elephants was waiting on the other side.

Maisy smiled through the pain as Joanie barreled into her, returning the little girl's hug. A second later, Maisy was released as Joanie spotted her mother. Leo immediately took Joanie's spot with a significantly more gentle grip. Maisy hugged the little boy back, seeing the other little boy, Ted, right behind him. Maisy held up her arm and Ted catapulted himself at her side as well. She let her arm drop around his shoulders and squeezed both boys tight for a moment.

"Everything's okay, guys," she told them. Two pairs of round eyes looked up at her.

"Really?" Leo asked.

"Really," Maisy answered firmly. "Let's go find your mom, okay?"

"Okay!" Leo agreed happily.

"It worked?" Maisy turned toward Lori's voice. She was hustling down the hall after the children, Joey in her arms.

"It worked!" Maisy said, smiling. Joey clapped in glee and held his arms out to Maisy. He and Lori grabbed onto her, and despite the ache in her face and side, the last of the tension finally eased from her body.

Lori pulled back and Joey clung to Maisy's shoulders. She supported his weight with an arm under his bottom, laughing as she looked down to see herself swamped by little boys. Joey laughed back at her and Maisy glanced around to see everyone smiling at his happiness, even Berta and Bill. The remaining members of Unit 7 looked tired, but at peace.

"I guess we should start opening up the cargo bay doors again," Sue said from beside Maisy, Joanie still wrapped around her middle. There were groans from the other passengers standing behind her.

"It can wait until tomorrow," Maisy smiled, patting the boys as they finally released her. She turned to encompass everyone in the hallway. "We did it. We still have a lot to figure out, but no more excitement for today."

There was a collective sigh and people began moving toward the cafeteria to celebrate.

Maisy turned to Sue, "Let's go check on Jane and see what the situation is on the bridge?"

"Sounds good." Sue smiled down at Joanie. "Want to see the bridge?"

"Yes, definitely!" the little girl responded.

"Is that where my mom is?" asked Leo.

"Yes!" Maisy put a hand on his shoulder. "Let's go find her."

18

A Brave New World

Stepping up to the closed bridge door with Joey still on her hip, Maisy tapped the panel. "Jane, it's us. We're all clear."

The door opened instantly and Jane appeared, her face relieved as she took in the group assembled in the hallway. Leo launched himself at his mother, clinging tightly to her waist and she wrapped an arm around his shoulders. "I had to shut down one of the engines," she said in a rush. "And I saw the emergency pod launch."

"Three of the marines left—" Maisy said.

"You shut down number five?" Tal asked at the same time. When Jane nodded, Tal sighed in relief. "That's good. Thank you."

"Three of the marines chose to stay with us. You've met Tal," Maisy gestured at the young man behind her. "This is Bill, our pilot," she said, "and Berta, the first officer." The two stepped forward and shook Jane's hand.

"I'm so glad you decided to stay," Jane told them sincerely.

"They didn't just leave," Sue said, entering the bridge. "Maisy kicked their sorry butts out!" She cackled with satisfaction.

"Well, Joe decided to leave on his own." Maisy shrugged.

"He was the other member of your dad's crew?" Jane asked.

"Yes," Maisy said quietly.

"It was his choice," Tal said, placing a hand tentatively on her shoulder.

Maisy nodded, burying her nose in Joey's soft hair. Lori approached from the other side, touching Maisy's arm.

"Maisy totally coldcocked the captain, though," Tal announced, chuckling. Lori burst out laughing.

"Seriously?" Jane asked.

"Seriously!" Sue confirmed. "She laid that old fart flat out on the floor."

Lori and Jane and the children demanded to hear all of the details of the epic battle and Sue and Tal told the story with glee, despite Maisy's objections. Even Berta threw in some details, obviously not at all upset to have seen Tratt and Rosa trussed up and pitched off the ship like yesterday's trash.

After the third rehashing of the fight, Maisy finally called it a day. "Okay, everyone needs to get some rest. Tomorrow we start figuring out our next steps."

"I'll take first watch," Tal offered.

"I'll sit with you for a while." Jane stepped up. "And you can run me through the bridge procedures."

"Okay," Tal agreed.

"Let's meet tomorrow and make sure that the four of us have access to all of the ship's systems," Maisy suggested. "We can also see if any of the other passengers are interested in assuming bridge duties." Maisy gazed around the bridge, at the empty consoles. "This ship must have had a crew at least twice this size."

Berta nodded in agreement. "Yes, it's been difficult keeping the ship running with just six crew."

"Speaking of running," Maisy segued, "what is the situation with the engines? We all heard the emergency shutdown warning."

"It's not as serious as it sounds," Tal reassured them. "It may take me a couple of days to get these two back up and running, but they're mechanically sound. I might even be able to get us another engine. Number two looks promising." Tal explained about the coolant issue and outlined the procedure he'd need to follow to reclaim it from the damaged engines.

"Well, that was better than I was expecting. Let's talk tomorrow and I can try to help you with the repairs," Maisy suggested. "But for now, it's time to call it a day.

Saying their goodnights, Maisy and her friends continued to the elevator. Stepping inside, Joey reached for Lori and Maisy handed the little boy off. Yawning, he rested his head on his sister's shoulder as the elevator took them down.

As they stepped off, there were still some people milling around the corridors and they took a moment to chat with them, explaining the engine issue. "We'll post an update to the board and we'll definitely keep meeting every night in the cafeteria," Maisy told them. "We're all in this together now. Go get some sleep and we'll talk tomorrow."

Back in their suite, Maisy collapsed onto the bench and leaned her head back against the wall, eyes closed.

"You've got a little blood here," Lori said, pressing a damp towel against Maisy's head.

"It's fine," Maisy dismissed, but she let Lori fuss over her. Carefully Maisy lifted her t-shirt to reveal the purpled skin of her ribcage.

"Oh, Maze!" Lori cried.

"It really is okay," Maisy reassured her. "Although, I'm sure tomorrow morning I'm going to feel like I was run over by a bus."

Sue came over, a coldpack in her hands. "Put this against your cheek, Maze." Sue pressed the pack against Maisy's bruised face, holding it in place until she obediently took it. "We need to wrap those ribs. Let me find something." Sue disappeared into her bedroom and returned a moment later with a sheet. She tore long strips off of one end and made Maisy lift her shirt so she and Lori could wrap her ribs tightly.

"Why do I feel like I'm getting ready for the ball?" Maisy asked. The three of them broke into laughter, exhaustion giving way to hysteria. It hurt to laugh but Maisy knew they all needed it. Her ribs finally bound, she stood limply between the two women. Their laughter had petered out but they were all still smiling.

Across the room, the children were sitting in Joey's makeshift enclosure, playing an intricate game involving a case of flexiplas plumbing fittings that Lori had found in the cargo bay.

Her eyes on the children, Sue said softly, "We could go home, you know."

"Home?" Maisy asked, lowering her shirt over her bandages and settling carefully back onto the bench.

Lori sat down beside Maisy, her eyes on Sue. "Earth, you mean?"

Sue nodded. "Certainly not the Citadel. That was never home and they've made it clear we aren't welcome back." Sue frowned, the last few weeks of uncertainty and fear still fresh.

Lori's face hardened. "Going back to the station isn't an option for any of us." Maisy touched the other girl's arm. She'd lost so much. "But Earth doesn't really feel like home either," Lori continued. "I barely remember Earth, honestly."

"Earth abandoned us before the Citadel did. If the coalition government wouldn't have pulled out of the rim, leaving us at the mercy of the pirates and the corporation..." Maisy trailed off, not finishing her thought. *Lori's parents would be alive. My dad would be alive.*

"Is that what you want, Sue?" Maisy asked. "To go to Earth?" Maisy wasn't sure if that was even possible, but it was an option she hadn't considered. It was certainly closer than 761.

"I've been thinking about it," Sue admitted. "We could just turn this ship around and head in system." Sue sat down on the bench beside Lori and Maisy, the three of them watching the children. "It wouldn't be easy," Sue continued. "We'd have to go through the same area where this ship was originally shot up. It would be a long trip."

"We'd have to worry about the CSS, not just pirates. Everyone would be gunning for us," Maisy pointed out.

Lori sighed. "Even if we made it to Earth, Joey and I don't have anyone there. Do you guys have family there?"

"I don't," Maisy said.

"No, we don't either," admitted Sue. "We came out to the rim because there wasn't anything there for us." She sighed.

"We'll figure things out tomorrow," Maisy told her. "Let's get some sleep."

Sue nodded, patting Maisy's knee as she drew herself to her feet and walked over to the children's makeshift fort.

"Time for bed, guys," Sue told them firmly, ignoring their half-hearted protests.

A ping from the door changed Sue's path and she veered toward the entrance to the suite. Despite how well the day had gone, everyone tensed as she opened the door. They all breathed a sigh of relief at the sight of Jane waiting on the other side. Leo launched himself up from the floor and gave his mom a fierce hug.

"We were all just heading to bed," Sue told Jane as she moved into the room, Leo attached like a barnacle.

"Brilliant idea," Jane smiled.

Maisy pushed herself to her feet. "Everything went well on the bridge?" she asked.

"Yes," Jane answered. "Your Tal is a smart guy. I learned a lot. I can walk you through it all tomorrow."

"Excellent." Maisy said. "I'll see you in the morning." Maisy turned toward the bedroom, her bruises aching. There were undoubtedly pain blockers somewhere on the ship, but she was too tired to look for them now. Pausing at the doorway to the bedroom, Maisy looked back. Sue had resumed hustling the children off to bed, Lori was sitting on the bench Maisy had just left, deep in thought, and Jane was crossing to the kitchen unit.

Thank you, Maisy thought, before turning back to the bed-room and slipping out of the room.

19

Your updated itinerary

Maisy Renner knew she was dreaming when her suit began to melt. She was floating through space, stars spinning slowly around her as her space suit dripped away. Soon, there was nothing left, just her naked body. The emptiness of space was pleasantly cool against her skin and her body was relaxed as it hung, weightless, in the void. The stars smiled at her as Maisy floated patiently, searching the great, windless sky for 761.

There was a planet below her and in her dream Maisy recognized it as home. *Strange*, Maisy thought. *Strange home. But home should be familiar.* As if she were walking into a picture, Maisy was able to step onto the surface of the planet. She stood there, still naked, and the sun warmed her skin. As she walked over the short, soft grass, geometric shapes appeared on the surface and she followed them to the top of a small rise.

On the other side of the hill, the land dropped off abruptly, creating a cliff overlooking a small valley. On the floor of the valley below, small white houses grew up out of the ground like mushrooms.

Maisy turned her back on the valley and walked back down the hill to where she'd first stepped onto the planet. She was surprised to see the shuttle from the cargo bay sitting in the spot, its ramp lowered and the interior in shadow. As Maisy approached the ship, figures took shape in the darkness.

Maisy opened her eyes without moving any other part of her body.

She recognized the room she shared with Lori and Joey immediately. Her ears picked out the slight shuffling sighs of Joey's breathing coming from across the room. Maisy rolled over carefully and picked out Lori's shape in the darkness. Her breathing was soft and even and Maisy knew she was still asleep. Judging from the lighting level, Maisy guessed it was about 0600.

It was going to be a long day. They would need to gather all of the passengers of the *Oro* and start making plans for the future. Nothing was set in stone. As Sue had suggested the previous night, they could turn the ship back toward Earth. They could continue toward 761 or find a completely different planet.

Maisy wasn't sure exactly what the future would bring, but she knew her life was changing, yet again. The difference was that this time, she wasn't alone. It was time for Maisy to build a new life, far from Earth.

About Author

Michael Owens is a single mom, dog rescuer, teacher, designer, user advocate, consultant, and many, many other things. She lives by the sea with her beautiful daughter and an astonishingly lazy pack of borzoi, greyhounds, and chihuahuas.

For more works by Michael and the other amazing authors of Pepperback Press, please visit PepperbackPress.com.

HTTP://PEPPERBACKPRESS.COM